The
Bears' Famous
Invasion *of* Sicily

The
Bears' Famous
Invasion *of* Sicily

Written and illustrated by
DINO BUZZATI

Translated from the Italian by
FRANCES LOBB

*With an introduction
and reader's companion by*
LEMONY SNICKET

🏛 HarperTrophy®
An Imprint of HarperCollins*Publishers*

Harper Trophy® is a registered trademark of
HarperCollins Publishers Inc.

The Bears' Famous Invasion of Sicily
Copyright © Dino Buzzati Estate, published in Italy
by Arnoldo Mondadori Editore
Introduction and Reader's Companion
© 2005 by Lemony Snicket

First published in Italian as
La famosa invasione degli orsi in Sicilia
Published in the United States of America by
The New York Review of Books, 2003
Published by arrangement with
The New York Review of Books

Library of Congress Cataloging-in-Publication Data
Buzzati, Dino, 1906–1972.
[Famosa invasione degli orsi in Sicilia. English]
The bears' famous invasion of Sicily / written and illustrated by Dino
Buzzati ; translated from the Italian by Frances Lobb ; introduction and
reader's companion by Lemony Snicket.— 1st Harper Trophy ed.
     p.   cm.
Summary: In search of food, Leander, King of the Bears, leads his
subjects from their safe caves in the mountains of Sicily to the valley where
they triumph over many enemies.
     ISBN 0-06-072608-3 (pbk.)
[1. Fairy tales. 2. Bears—Fiction. 3. Kings, queens, rulers, etc.—Fiction.
4. Sicily (Italy)—Fiction. 5. Italy--Fiction.] I. Lobb, Frances. II. Snicket,
Lemony. III. Title.
PZ8.B965Be 2004
[Fic]—dc22   2004013206
                                                                    CIP
                                                                     AC

❖
First Harper Trophy edition, 2005
Visit us on the World Wide Web!
www.harperchildrens.com

INTRODUCTION BY
LEMONY SNICKET

An introduction at the start of a book is like a swordfight at the start of a meal, because no one likes to participate in such a thing when it is time to sit down. If you are interested in reading Dino Buzzati's *The Bears' Famous Invasion of Sicily,* it is best to simply ignore this introduction, turn the page, and begin.

When you are finished, if you are interested in further discussions of this book, you may turn to the Reader's Companion, which is hidden in the back of the book. If you are not interested, don't.

The Bears' Famous Invasion *of* Sicily

 Once upon a time, in the ancient mountains of Sicily, two hunters captured the bear-cub Tony, son of Leander, King of the Bears. But this occurred some years before our story begins.

Characters

KING LEANDER. He is the King of the Bears, the son of a King who in turn had a King as father. He is therefore a bear of most ancient lineage. He is tall, strong, valiant, virtuous, and intelligent too, though not as intelligent as all that. We hope you will like him. His coat is magnificent and he is justly proud of it. Faults? Perhaps he is a little too credulous, and in certain circumstances he will show himself somewhat over-ambitious. He wears no crown upon his head but may be distinguished from the rest both by his general appearance and by the fact that he carries a great sword suspended from a tricolour scarf. He will live for ever as the leader of his beasts in the invasion of Sicily; at least, he should.

TONY. King Leander's little son. There is little to be said about him. He was still extremely small when two unknown hunters captured him in the mountains and bore him down to the plains. Since that time nothing has been heard of him. Who knows what has happened to him?

THE GRAND DUKE. Tyrant of all Sicily and sworn enemy of the bears. He is extraordinarily vain, and changes his clothes eight times a day, but in spite of this he never succeeds in looking less hideous than he is. Children laugh at him behind his back because of his large, hooked nose. But woe to them if he ever discovers this.

11

PROFESSOR AMBROSE. A most important personage, whose name you would do well to learn at once. He was Court Astrologer, that is, in plain English, he studied the stars every night (unless it was cloudy), and according to their position foretold things to the Grand Duke before they came to pass; all this by means of very difficult calculations, or so he said. Naturally not all of them were successful; sometimes he hit the mark and sometimes he did not; and then there was trouble. By guessing right he recently put the Grand Duke in a tremendous rage — we shall see why, later — and was expelled from the palace with ignominy. As well as this, Ambrose claims to be a magician and to know how to work spells, but so far he has never worked any. He does in fact own a magic wand which he guards exceedingly jealously and which he has never used. Indeed, it appears that this wand can only be used twice, after which its power is exhausted and it can be thrown away in the dustbin. What does Professor Ambrose look like? He is very tall, and lanky, with a long pointed beard. On his head he wears an enormous top hat, over his shoulders a very old greatcoat, greasy and dirty. Is he a good man? Is he a bad man? That you must judge for yourselves.

THE BEAR SALTPETRE. One of the most eminent bears, and a friend of King Leander. He is very handsome and a great favourite with the she-bears. He is always elegant, is a distinguished orator, and would like to rise to high office in the State. But with what high office can King Leander ever entrust him amid the solitude of the bleak mountains? No, he was not made for a harsh life among the rocks and snows; Saltpetre would feel at home only in the great world, amid receptions, balls and banquets!

THE BEAR TITAN. A giant, perhaps the biggest of them all. They say he is a whole head taller than King Leander himself, and moreover he is very valiant in war. Without his providential intervention, the invasion of Sicily would have ended in utter disaster on the very first day.

12

THE BEAR THEOPHILUS. He is the wisest of them all. Growing old has taught him many things. King Leander frequently asks his advice. In our story he will appear only for a few moments, and then, as you will see, not in flesh and blood. But he is such an excellent bear that it would be wicked not to mention him.

THE BEAR MERLIN. Of humble stock but noble disposition, and full of good will. He stands apart from the others, lost in marvellous dreams of battle and renown. Will these ever come true? Unless we are much mistaken, more will be heard of him one day.

THE BEAR MARZIPAN. Of undistinguished appearance, but worthy of admiration for his ingenuity. He spends his time in inventing a quantity of machines and devices which are undoubtedly brilliant; but the necessary materials are lacking in the mountains, so until now he has not been able to put anything remarkable into practice. In the future, however, who knows?

THE BEAR DANDELION. Gifted with rare powers of observation, he can discover things which people more learned than he fail to recognise. One fine day he will become a kind of amateur detective. He is a worthy beast, and one can have complete confidence in him.

COUNT MOLFETTA. A noble of some importance, cousin and ally of the Grand Duke. He has at his disposal a truly strange and terrible army, such as no other ruler possesses. At present we will say no more; and it is useless to press us.

TROLL. A wicked old ogre who lives in Three Peak Castle. He feeds preferably on human flesh, the more tender the better, but he eats bears too, of course. Old and solitary as he is, he would probably not succeed in procuring any by himself; but in his service, and charged with this very task, is Marmoset the Cat in person.

13

MARMOSET THE CAT. A fabulous and most ferocious monster. We think it best not to speak of him at length here. You will be frightened enough when he suddenly appears on the scene. There is no point in being frightened now. « Bad news will keep », as the bear Theophilus said, bless him.

THE SEA SERPENT. Another monster still more gigantic and no less perilous. To make up for this, however, he is a great deal cleaner, since he lives in the water all the time. He has the body of a serpent, as his name implies, but with the head and teeth of a dragon.

THE WEREWOLF. A third monster. It is possible that he may not appear in our story. In fact, as far as we know he has never appeared anywhere, but one never knows. He might suddenly appear from one moment to the next, and then how foolish we should look for not having mentioned him.

VARIOUS APPARITIONS. Ugly but harmless. They are the ghosts of dead men and bears. It is difficult to tell one from the other. In fact, when they are turned into ghosts, bears lose their coats, and their noses get shorter, so that they differ little from human ghosts although the ghosts of bears are a trifle plumper. In our story the very small ghost of an old clock will also appear.

THE OLD MAN OF THE MOUNTAINS. A most powerful spirit of the rocks and glaciers, of an irascible temperament. None of us has ever seen him, and nobody knows exactly where he lives, but we may be sure that he exists. For that reason it is always better to speak civilly of him.

14

A SCREECH-OWL. We shall hear his voice for a moment in Chapter Two. As he is hidden in the depths of the forest, we shall not be able to see him, the more so as dusk will already have fallen. For that reason the portrait printed here is completely imaginary. The screech-owl will merely give one of his melancholy hoots, as we have said. And that is all.

The Scene

First we shall see the majestic mountains of Sicily, though there are no longer any mountains in Sicily (so many, many years have passed since then!). They are all covered in snow.

Next we shall descend to the verdant valley with its villages, streams, woods full of small birds, and houses scattered here and there; a most beautiful landscape. But on each side of the valley the mountains still tower, not so high and steep as those we first saw, but also full of perils; there are for instance enchanted castles, dens with venomous dragons, other castles inhabited by ogres and so on. In short, there is always something to beware of, especially at night.

Then, little by little we shall approach the fabulous capital of Sicily, of which today not even a memory remains (so many years have gone by!). It is surrounded by very high walls and fortified strongholds. The chief stronghold is called Cormorant Castle. What things we shall see there!

At last we shall enter the capital, famous all over the world for its palaces of yellow marble, its towers which touch the sky, its churches overlaid with gold, its gardens in perpetual bloom, its equestrian circuses, its amusement parks and its theatres. The Grand Theatre Excelsior is the finest of all.

And what of the mountains we first left? Shall we ever return to our ancient mountains?

Chapter **1**

Sit still as mice on this occasion
And listen to the Bears' Invasion
Of Sicily, a long, long while
Ago when beasts were good, men vile.

Then Sicily, unlike today,
Was formed in quite another way.
Her snow-clad mountains rose so high
That with their peaks they touched the sky,
With sometimes in the mountains' stead,
Volcanoes, shaped like loaves of bread;
And one had a peculiar manner
Of puffing smoke out like a banner;
It used to roar like one possessed
And even today it is still rumbling away with the best.

There in the gloomy mountain lairs
Above the snowline lived the bears,
And they fed on lichen and truffles and fungi
And chestnuts and berries and never went hungry.

Very well, then. Many years earlier, when Leander, King of the Bears, was looking for fungi on the mountains with his little son Tony, two hunters had stolen his child from him. The father had wandered along a steep crag for a moment and they had surprised the cub alone and defenceless, had tied him up like a parcel and lowered him down the precipices, down to the valley at the bottom.

« Tony! Tony! » loud he cried,
But vainly did he waste his breath;
Only the echoes still replied,
Around a silence as of death.
He sought him up, he sought him down.
Could they have taken him to the town?

Eventually the King had returned to his lair and said that his son had fallen off a crag and been killed. He had not had the courage to tell the truth, which would have been a disgrace for any bear, let alone the King. After all, he had allowed the cub to be stolen from him.

From that day onwards he had known no peace. How many times he had thought of going down among men to look for his son! But what could he do by himself, a bear among men? They would have killed him, or chained him up, and that would have been the end of him. And so the years went by.

Then there came a winter more terrible than any of the other winters. It was so cold that even the bears shivered under their heavy fur. Thick snow covered all the small plants, and there was nothing left to eat. They were so hungry that the smallest

22

The bears, driven by cold and hunger, go down to the plains and engage in battle with the seasoned troops of the Grand Duke sent to repulse them. The intrepidity of the bear Titan puts the Grand Ducal soldiers to flight.

cubs and the bears with weak nerves used to cry all night. They could not stand it any longer. At length one of them said : « Why don't we go down to the plains? ». In the clear morning light they could see the bottom of the valley free of snow, with human habitations, and smoke coming out of the chimneys, a sign that something was being prepared to eat. It seemed as if Paradise itself were down there. And the bears from their high crags remained for hours gazing at it and heaving deep sighs.

« Let us go down to the plains. Better fight with men than die of hunger up here,» said the more venturesome bears. And to tell the truth, the idea did not displease their king, Leander; it would be a good opportunity of looking for his little son. The danger would be far less if all his people descended in a body. Men would think twice before confronting such an army.

None of the bears, King Leander included, knew what men were really like, how wicked and cunning they were, what terrible weapons they possessed, or what traps they could invent to capture animals. So they decided to forsake the mountains and go down to the plains.

> When our tale begins, the Grand
> Duke was ruler of the land.
> Ugly, thin, conceited, grim,
> We shall hear some more of him.
> Who could ever be aspirant
> For the love of such a tyrant?

Now you must know that some months earlier the Court Astrologer, Professor Ambrose, had prophesied that an invincible force would come down from the mountains, that the Grand Duke would be put to rout, and that the enemy would make themselves masters of the whole country.

The Professor had said that, because he was sure of his facts, thanks to his calculations by the stars. But think of the Grand Duke! He fell into a passion and ordered the astrologer to be flogged and banished from Court. However, as he was superstitious, he ordered his soldiers to climb up the mountain sides and kill every living thing they found. Thus, he thought, nobody would be left in the mountains and so no one would be able to come down from them to conquer his kingdom.

Off went the soldiers, armed to the teeth, and they killed without mercy every living thing they encountered up there, old woodcutters, shepherd boys, squirrels, marmots, and even innocent little birds. Only the bears escaped, hidden in the deepest caves, and so did the Old Man of the Mountains, that grand, mysterious old man who will never die, and who lives no one has ever quite known where.

> But one night in haste a messenger cried
> « A snake has been seen on the mountain side! »
> And a serpent appeared, made of little black dots,
> He-bears and she-bears and bear tiny tots.
> « Bears? » laughed the Duke, « Just leave them to me,
> And soon you will see a great victory! »
> And then there was heard a fanfaronade
> As the Grand Ducal army came out on parade.
> « Forward, you dogs! Quick march, you cattle!
> Tomorrow at dawn we go forth to battle! »

26

The great encounter may be described
In the coloured print on the other side.
The bears above, as on the plan.
The Duke below. And the slaughter began.

For what could bears do, armed with arrows and spears
[and such trifles
Against culverin, cannon and grapeshot, and muskets
[and rifles?
The rifles crack, the unsullied snow turns red;
Who'll dig a grave to hold so many dead?

The Duke upon a sheltered slope
Observes it through a telescope,
While the courtiers to show how victorious their team is
Have painted his lens with a bear "in extremis",
So wherever he looks as the bloodshed increases
He sees only animals cut into pieces.
« Tell me, Your Excellence, what do you see? »
« A bear with his leg chopped off at the knee. »
« And now, Your Excellence, what see you there? »
« Nothing but dead bears everywhere. »
And the Duke in a state of the utmost delight
Hands out medals and titles to left and to right.
« Wonderful! Splendid! » says he, « Carry right on! »
He reckoned without the great bear Titan...

In fact, careless of danger, the bear Titan, with his gigantic
limbs and dauntless courage had climbed up a dizzy crag to-

gether with a few other bears worthy to accompany him and, having gained the top, was making enormous snowballs which he hurled down like avalanches on the troops of the Grand Duke.

With a heavy thud the white projectiles hurtled down, right in the midst of the Grand Ducal army. Wherever they fell, the terrible masses of snow made a clean sweep.

Fear, havoc and ruin to such an extent
May well terrify the Duke's regiment.
The troops run hither and thither, and shout:
« The Old Man of the Mountains has put us to rout! »
The bombardment of avalanches has told,
And has made the soldiers' blood run cold.
Take flight! Take flight! for who will stop you?
When fear once starts it gets atop you,
And once a panic is on the wing,
No one is left to halt the thing.
Worms devour the slain,
The Grand Duke rages in vain.
The bears are victorious though gory,
And the Battle ends in glory.

Chapter 2

If you carefully follow the plan
Depicting the battle scene,
You will notice a curious man
Away to the left in green.
This was Professor Ambrose,
Behind where the Duke's oriflamb rose.

Now tell us pray, Professor, about your magic powers;
And whether, if you wish, you could turn pebbles into flowers,
And flowers into precious stones, ruby and emerald posies,
And skunks and rats and warthogs into scented, crimson
[roses?
Gone are the days of old
When King Arthur was alive,
And a wand turned all to gold
And made all the people thrive.

The Professor can wave his wand
But twice ere its power flies,
And when he has woven the spells
Its magic forever dies.

31

Useless is dragon's gizzard,
Or beak of raven boiled,
Two spells, and then all is spoiled,
And the wizard no more a wizard.

But Ambrose is haunted still
By a fear of becoming ill,
And he jealously guards each spell
To save it for making him well.

He might live at ease, have a lot
Of money, do nothing but play,
Or eat seventeen times a day
But for these things he cares not a jot.

And now that we have made that plain,
Let us resume our tale again.

When the Grand Duke's army went forth to war against the bears, Ambrose had asked himself whether this would not be a good opportunity to regain favour with the tyrant and get himself recalled to court. It would be enough for him to use one of his spells and the bears would be decimated, and the Grand Duke would erect a statue to him. For that reason he wandered about unseen near the battle, ready to intervene at the right moment.

But the discomfiture of the Grand Duke had been so unexpected that it took even the wizard by surprise. By the time he had drawn his magic wand out of his pocket to rescue the

Count Molfetta's fighting boars attack the bears unexpectedly, but Ambrose the astrologer transforms them by a spell into balloons, gently rocked by the breeze. Hence the famous legend of Molfetta's flying boars.

Grand Duke, the bears were well over the mountains shouting for victory, and the Grand Duke had given it up as hopeless. So then the wizard paused with his wand in mid air, struck by a new thought. « Why should I help that vile Grand Duke who drove me out like a dog? » meditated the Professor. « Why should I not instead become a friend of the bears, who are sure to be great simpletons? Why should I not make them nominate me minister? With the bears I need not waste my spells, I need only say a few difficult words and they will remain agape like so many idiots. What an opportunity! »

Then he put his wand back again, and in the evening, when the victorious bears had encamped in a wood to feast on the provisions abandoned by the Grand Duke in his flight, when the moon rose behind the pine trees, sweetly lighting the meadows (for at the foot of the valley there was no more snow), when in the solitude of the countryside they began to hear the melancholy hooting of the screech owl, Professor Ambrose took courage, went down towards the bears and presented himself to King Leander.

Listen now to how he spoke, and to the wisdom which came from his lips.

He explained that he was a wizard, a necromancer (which is the same thing), a diviner, a prophet and a sorcerer. He said that he could work white magic and black magic, that he could read the stars, in short that he knew a great quantity of extraordinary things.

« Good, » replied King Leander very cordially. « I am really delighted that you came, because now you will be able to find my young son for me. »

35

« And where is this son of yours? » asked the wizard, realising that all was not going to be as simple as he had imagined.

« Wretch! » exclaimed King Leander, « If I knew, what need should I have to ask of you? »

« In short, you would like a spell? » stuttered the Professor, abashed.

« Of course I want a spell! And what bother can such a little thing be to a great sage like yourself? I am not asking you for the moon, after all! »

« Your Majesty, » begged Ambrose then, forgetting all the airs he had just put on, « Your Majesty, do you want to ruin me? I can only work one spell, only one in my whole life! » (Here he was telling a flat lie.) « You must wish to ruin me! »

So they began to argue, Leander determined to discover the whereabouts of his son, the wizard determined not to yield. The bears, tired and replete, fell asleep, but these two continued arguing.

The moon rose high in the sky and began to descend the other side; and still the two continued arguing.

The night grew shorter, bit by bit, and still the discussion was not over.

Dawn broke and the King and the wizard were still arguing.

But since things in life always happen when they are least expected, so, in the first rays of the sun, a large black cloud emerged from behind a neighbouring hill, like an advancing army.

« The wild boars! » cried a sentinel posted on the outskirts of the wood.

« The wild boars? » said Leander surprised.

36

« The wild boars themselves! » replied the bear sentinel, conscientious like all good sentinels.

It was in fact the horde of wild boars of Count Molfetta, the Grand Duke's cousin, coming to the rescue. Instead of soldiers, this important noble had trained an army of huge, savage pigs to war, and these were very wild and extremely brave, and celebrated all over the world. The Count cracked his whip from the hilltop on which he was standing so as to be out of danger. And on came the terrible boars at the gallop, their tusks whistling in the wind!

Alas, the bears were still asleep. Scattered here and there about the wood, round the ashes of the fires where they had bivouacked, they were at that very moment dreaming the sweet dreams of morning, which are always the most beautiful. Even the trumpeter was asleep and could not sound the alarm. In his trumpet, abandoned on the grass, the fresh woodland breeze whispered gently, sending forth delicate little notes, a subtle sound, and certainly not enough to wake the animals.

With Leander there was only a small band of bear fusiliers; they were the sentinels, armed with the fire-arms taken from the Grand Duke. There was no one else.

The boars lowered their heads and charged.

« And now? » stammered Professor Ambrose.

« Can't you see? » said King Leander with a certain bitterness. « We are alone. And now we must die. Let us at least strive to die decently! » (and he drew his sword from his scabbard.) « Let us die like gallant soldiers! »

« And what about me? » begged the astrologer, « what about me? »

Must he, Ambrose, die too? And for such a stupid reason? He really did not wish to do so at all. But the wild boars were only a few hundred yards away and they came on like a river in spate.

And then the wizard plunged his hand into his pocket, drew out the magic wand, pronounced a few strange words under his breath and traced some signs in the air. Oh, how easy it was to cast a spell when one was as frightened as that!

And behold, one of the wild boars, the foremost and biggest of them all, suddenly left the ground and swelled and swelled, gradually turning into a real, true balloon; a beautiful air balloon which floated up into the sky. Then a second followed, and then a third and then a fourth.

As fast as they arrived the fatal boars were mysteriously bewitched, and they swelled up like footballs.

Gracious! How they floated away, away with the breezes and the little birds, up among the clouds, gently rocked by the winds!

Fate had willed it thus. The first of the spells had had to be spent, and only one remained to Ambrose. One more stroke of the magic wand and he would become a man as other men again, old and ugly into the bargain. What had been the good of so much parsimony?

Meanwhile, however, his spell had saved the bears. The last wild boar vanished till nothing remained but a tiny black speck high in the face of the heavens.

Hence the legends, which caused such uproars,
Of Count Molfetta's flying boars.

38

Chapter 3

In the neighbourhood there was an old castle, in fact at that time there were many old castles, but the one we mean is Demon Castle, which was all in ruins, and hideous, and full of wild beasts, but which was the most famous because it was inhabited by ghosts. As you very well know, all old castles are generally haunted by a ghost or, at most, by two or three. But in Demon Castle there were so many that you could not count them. There were hundreds of them, if not thousands, lying hid by day; there were even ghosts in the keyholes.

There are some mothers who say: « I cannot imagine what pleasure people get out of telling children ghost stories: it terrifies them, and afterwards at night they start screaming if they hear a mouse. » Perhaps the mothers are right. Still, there are three things to remember. First of all, ghosts, always supposing they exist, have never done children any harm, in fact they have never done anyone any harm, it is simply that people insist on getting frightened. Ghosts and spirits, if they exist, (and today they have almost vanished off the face of the earth) are natural and innocent things like the wind, or the rain, or shadows of trees, or the voice of the cuckoo in the evening; and they are probably sad at having to live all by themselves in dreary, old, uninhabited houses; and they are probably afraid of people as they hardly ever see them, and perhaps if we showed a little more confidence they would become friendly, and would enjoy playing with us at, say, Hide and Seek.

Secondly, Demon Castle does not exist any more, the Grand Duke's city does not exist any more, there are no more bears in Sicily, and the whole story is now so remote that there is no cause for alarm.

Thirdly, that is how the story was, and we cannot alter it.

> Silent, gloomy, dark and bleak
> The Castle jutted from its peak,
> And superstition and misinformation
> Gave it a sinister reputation.
> If you slept there, they said, all night,
> When morning came you were dead of fright.
> Apparitions, spirits, spectres, phantoms and ghosts
> Came by night in hosts!

Even Sparrow, the famous brigand, who used to boast that he was not afraid even of God, was found there as dead as a doornail. The fact is that he was bold and powerful when he was surrounded by his cut-throats or when he was drunk. But in a ruined and deserted mansion, without an innkeeper to whom to joke and keep his courage up, finding himself all alone for the first time, Sparrow began to think about his past. He suddenly remembered all the dirty tricks he had played, and he was already feeling more uncomfortable than he had ever felt, when the ghosts of two old boatmen whom he had

42

Professor Ambrose lures the bears to the terrifying Demon Castle, inhabited by ghosts, so that they shall die of terror. How could he have dreamed that all would end in a party with music, songs, waltzes and minuets, among the ruins?

formerly assassinated passed casually by him. The two ghosts did not even look at him, did not even deign to notice his presence, but the brigand's terror was such as to deprive him of breath once and for all. And from that day onwards, people could walk the streets at night again without fear of assault.

Now Professor Ambrose, in a great rage with King Leander and the bears for obliging him to waste one of his two available spells, determined to be revenged. He thought it would be a magnificent idea to lure the animals to Demon Castle. There, simple creatures that they were, the bears would certainly fall dead on the spot at the sight of ghosts.

No sooner said than done. Ambrose advised King Leander to lead his animals to the castle that very night, for they would find a place to sleep, eat and amuse themselves. « Meanwhile I shall go on ahead and make the necessary preparations. »

And he ran on ahead to the castle to warn the ghosts. As a wizard, he was quite at home with spirits, knew perfectly well that they were not dangerous, and did not stand on ceremony with them.

« Come on, come on, my friends! » shouted the Professor, running through the deserted rooms, on which dusk was already descending. « Wake up, you have got guests! »

And out of dusty hangings, out of rusty armour, out of sooty fireplaces, out of old books, out of bottles, even out of the pipes of the organ in the chapel, hurried the ghosts; and to tell the truth they were ugly creatures, and anything but prepossessing to people who were not used to them. But Ambrose himself thought nothing of it; he was quite at home there.

The next thing he did was to pick up some bellows,
And with huffings and puffings and ho, there's! and hellos!
And stirrings and proddings in nooks and crannies,
He woke the old spirits of granddads and grannies.
« Make haste now, please, Countess, » he whispered, « for now
« You must waken from slumber to hiss and miaow.
« You too, in the corner, my most noble lords,
« Come forth when I ask you without further words.
« Our programme tonight must be extra frightening
« Chains clanking, teeth gnashing, and thunder and lightning.
« You do your worst and I'll be bystander,
« And the fright of it all will kill King Leander. »

It was the witching hour of midnight! From the topmost tower, the ghost of the grandfather clock long ago in pieces sent forth twelve quavering ding-dongs, and clouds of bats detached themselves from the crumbling rafters and swooped about the castle. At that very moment King Leander, at the head of his people, was advancing through the deserted corridors, astonished to find neither lighted lamps nor laden tables, nor an orchestra (as Ambrose had promised).

No, you wouldn't say it was an orchestra! From a huge spider's web hanging in the corner there appeared a dozen ghosts, who advanced on King Leander roaring and making faces.

Ambrose had thought that the bears, who were simple beasts, would be frightened to death. But he had made a mistake. Just because they were simple and frank, the bears regarded these strange apparitions with curiosity and nothing more. What was

46

there to be afraid of? They had neither teeth nor fangs nor claws. And they had voices like screech-owls.

« Oh, look at the white sheets dancing by themselves! » exclaimed a little bear.

« And you, you pretty handkerchief, why are you spinning round like that? » said another beast to a pale little ghost who was twirling round just in front of his muzzle.

But suddenly the spirits came to a halt, and ceased roaring and grimacing.

« What do I see? » cried one of them in a hollow but anxious voice, changing his tone completely. « It is our worthy King Leander! Don't you recognise me? »

« Well, I really... I don't know... » stammered Leander. « I am Theophilus, » said the spirit, « and there — » pointing to his companions, « are Gideon, Boris, Smallpaws and Aquiline, your faithful bears. Do you not know them? »

And at last the King recognised them; they were his bears who had fallen in battle and already had been changed into ghosts. They had taken refuge in the castle, and had at once become friends with the ghosts of humans, with whom they lived happily together. But how they had changed! Where, now, were their charming muzzles, their powerful paws, their sumptuous fur coats? They had become transparent, soft, pale, evanescent wisps of veiling!

« My brave bears! » said Leander, much moved. And he clasped their paws.

They embraced, or at least they tried to embrace, for it is no easy thing for a beast made of flesh and blood and a ghost made of impalpable stuff to do. Meanwhile more bears had arrived

47

from one direction, more ghosts from another. New encounters took place amid bursts of laughter and joyous exclamations. The ghosts of humans, too, once the first shyness had worn off, received them royally. It hardly seemed true to the ghosts that at last a time had come for them to have a little fun. They lit bonfires and without more ado began dancing to the sound of an improvised band; there was a violincello, a violin and a flute, to say nothing of singers and ballet dancers.

And what about Ambrose? Why was he not to be seen? He was hiding in a dark corner and watching the scene from there, cursing the bears, and the stupidity of the spirits who had not succeeded in frightening them. But for tonight there was nothing to be done about it.

Bears and ghosts danced, sang and made friends. To crown their joy, a very old ghost succeeded in discovering, in the castle cellars, among piles of skeletons and enormous rats and mice, an ancient bottle of wine such as not even the Grand Duke could boast. Having, as King, taken part in the first round of drinking, Leander preferred to retire with the ghost of Theophilus who had been a wise and prudent bear. With him he discussed the situation at length and the possibilities of finding his kidnapped son once more.

« Ah, you mean your Tony, » said Theophilus at this point. « I forgot to tell you! Do you know I had news of him? You know he is at the T.... »

He was unable to finish the sentence. Ding, dong, ding went the ghost of the grandfather clock. Three in the morning! The hour when spells are broken! In a moment the ghosts had melted away like smoke from a chimney, and had turned into a light mist which lingered in the rooms a little with a faint rustling and then disappeared in its turn.

Leander could have wept with rage! To think that he had been on the point of learning where Tony was! But it could not be helped. It would have been useless to wait for the following night, because there is a law of the ghosts which decrees that they may only become visible once a year.

Chapter **4**

Little Tony, King Leander's son, was therefore « at the T.... » But what on earth did the T stand for? What was it that old Theophilus' ghost was going to say? Leander tried to guess. But so many words begin with T. At the Tournament? At the Tailor's? Theatre? Tropics? Tribunal? Table? Oh, it was no good going on. Or did Theophilus mean that Tony was « at the Termination » of something, at the Termination of his troubles, perhaps, or the termination of his life? (but that was a horrid thought). At last somebody said: « I wonder if the old bear meant to allude to Three Peak, the other castle round here? »

King Leander had never heard of it, but some of those bears who always know everything explained to him that Three Peak was a grim fortress at the base of a narrow pass between the Pilgrim Mountains, three or four leagues away. The fortress was inhabited by an ogre called Troll who lived there all by himself.

Could the Ogre have captured the bear-cub? The only thing to do was to go and see. So King Leander organised an expedition with a battalion.

The ogre was asleep. He was now old and spent his time in

53

bed, getting up only for a few minutes at mealtimes. As to his food, he had organised matters well. A long time ago, as you ought to know, he had succeeded in capturing the famous cat, Marmoset, who was nearly as big as a house. Marmoset the Cat was shut up in an enormous cage in the castle courtyard and forced to work for him.

Who among you has not heard tell of Marmoset the Cat? At one time he ravaged all Europe, devouring horses and men. Then the peasants fled to the mountains or barred themselves in their houses. Finally one day he came to the threshold of Three Peak, and there the ogre was lying in wait for him, with a huge net made of witches' hair. The cat was taken prisoner and shut up in the great cage.

And now to return to our story.

At the entrance to the pass the ogre had put up misleading signposts saying « To the Paradise Inn, food and lodging free, twenty minutes' walk, » or « Children! Free distribution of wonderful toys » with an arrow pointing the way, or else « Hunting forbidden, » and then of course hunters immediately went in that direction.

Thus travellers, disobedient children who ran about the countryside instead of going to school, and hunters in search of game ended up at Three Peak.

At this point the raven sentinels flew into the ogre's room and pecked him awake. Troll the ogre opened the trap door of Marmoset's cage, and Marmoset shot out a paw and crushed the passer-by. Finally Troll carefully picked out the most tender and tasty morsels, and threw the rest to Marmoset.

The ogre, then, was asleep. He had just gobbled up an ap-

54

petising little child called Johnnie Hardwinter, who was in the bottom class at school and who had played truant that morning. But in through the window at full speed came a raven, who flew to the ogre's bed and began pecking his nose with all its might.

« What are you doing, you wretch? » growled Troll, without even opening his eyes.

« There are visitors, sir, there are visitors, » croaked the raven.

« Bother! Can't they ever let me sleep in peace? » swore the ogre, leaping out of bed.

And whom did he see approaching along the narrow road hewn out of the side of the precipice? Travellers or children or hunters, or anything good to eat? It was Professor Ambrose all out of breath.

« Well, Death's head, » cried the ogre, who had known him for many years, « what ill fortune brings you here? »

« Wake up, Troll, » said the magician, now standing underneath the window. « The bears are coming! »

« Good, good, » replied the ogre. « Bear flesh is excellent. A little tough, perhaps, but full of flavour. How many are there — a couple? »

« No, you wouldn't say there were a couple, » sniggered the magician. « More than that. »

« Well, ten then? My cat will have a good feast. »

« No, you wouldn't say there were ten. » And Ambrose for a wonder burst out laughing.

« You infernal ruffian, will you please tell me? » shouted the ogre in a voice that made the mountains quake. « Tell me, how many are there? »

« A battalion, if you want to know. There must be two or three hundred of them. And they are coming to pay a call on you. »

« The Devil they are! » exclaimed Troll, impressed at last. « What had we better do, then? »

« Set your cat free. Open his cage. He will see to the arrangements all right. »

« Set Marmoset the Cat free? Supposing that afterwards he went off on his own affairs? » Still, the idea was excellent.

And there was no time to be lost, either. There at the bottom of the deep valley where the road began climbing up the side of the mountain a long file of black dots could be seen advancing, an endless file.

Troll went down to the courtyard and opened the cage.

It was a beautiful day. Panting a little the bears were climbing at a good pace. Then suddenly the sunbeams were blotted out as if by a sudden storm.

The bears raised their eyes.

Good heavens! It was not the darkness of a storm but the shadow of Marmoset the Cat leaping down from the crags.

Magpies gadflies
Glow-worms dogs
Bats rats
Slow-worms hogs
Chimpanzees caterpillars
Fleas armadillas
The appetite whet
Of Marmoset

In the deep gorge between the Pilgrim Mountains, the bears are attacked by Marmoset the Cat, thirsty for blood. Some fly, some fire shots in a vain attempt at defence, some hide, some leap into the abyss rather than end their days as a mouthful for the fabulous monster.

Jameses Johnses Adolfs Alphonses
Scullions sucklings dukes ducklings
Normans Nathaniels Davids Daniels
Spies doctors painters proctors
The appetite whet of Marmoset.

Carnage and blood,
Massacre, doom,
Earthquake and flood,
Slaughter, hecatomb,
The appetite whet
Of Marmoset.

The bears had never seen anything like it. Then, some cried for help. Some fled. Some tried to hide themselves and shrink into the crevices of the rock, some fired shots in a vain attempt at defence, some even lept into the abyss rather than end their days as a mouthful for the fabulous monster.

Only one kept his head. He was a bear of humble birth called Merlin, whom the majority had so far considered a simpleton because he was a little deaf. But this time there was no need of good hearing. When he saw Marmoset the Cat wreaking havoc among his comrades, Merlin took from a bag one of the large hand grenades captured from the Grand Duke, and, clasping it tightly in his paws, ran towards the monster's gaping mouth.

« Merlin, what are you doing, are you mad? » they cried, but he ran steadfastly on, straight into the jaws of death.

The cat did not even have to put out a paw for him but found him right under his nose and gulped him down ravenously, hair and hide. Down went Merlin, head over heels into the monster's stomach. When he got to the bottom he lit the fuse.

There was a blinding flash, an enormous black cloud, and a miaow that curdled the blood. For a moment all was confusion. Then the wind blew the smoke away, and the bears began to dance about like mad creatures, singing songs of triumph.

There at the foot of the precipice, Marmoset the Cat lay dead with his stomach torn open. And a little further on, all scorched and bruised, lay the gallant bear Merlin who had sacrificed himself for his comrades. The explosion had blown him right out of Marmoset's stomach, and by a stroke of luck he had landed in a great pool of water which softened his fall and put out his fur which was alight. He rose to his feet without aid, and even managed to walk alone. Bravo!

But now a voice could be heard crying: « Tony, my Tony! Where are you? » It was King Leander who had rushed into the fortress in the hope of finding his son. Crossing the courtyard, he searched room after room. But not a living soul was to be seen. The ogre and the magician had fled to the mountains. Of the bear-cub not a trace could be found. Everywhere there was silence and emptiness.

But alas! The sad fact had to be faced. How much suffering there had been, to no purpose! How many bears had died in vain!

Chapter 5

At the gates of the capital stood Cormorant Castle, the fortress of fortresses, the most powerful stronghold ever known at that time. The road leading to the city passed through it, but if the doors were shut, massive iron doors, no one could enter. Whole armies had attempted to do so, for months on end they had bivouacked at the gates of the capital and continued firing heavy cannon to pierce the walls, but all in vain. Exhausted and disappointed they had had to resign themselves to taking the road back again.

Now the Grand Duke had organised his defence within the castle and was as cool as a cucumber. The bears, indeed! If the bears should dare to make an attempt he would be very pleased, for mountains of projectiles were ready to be hurled at them. The sentinels on their beats on the ramparts marched up and down with their muskets on their shoulders. « Slope arms! » they cried in turn every half hour, and all was going beautifully.

But the bears were advancing through the valley singing their rough songs and thinking that their battles were over. The gates of the great city, so they thought, would be open to them, the people would come out to meet them carrying buns and jars

63

full of honey. Brave and worthy animals as they were! Why should men not immediately make friends with them?

And behold, one evening there appeared against the sky the towers and silver domes of the city, all illuminated, with its white palaces, and marvellous gardens; but before it, steep and terrifying as a precipice, rose the walls of the fortress. A sentinel saw them from a corner turret. « Who goes there? » he shouted at the top of his voice, and then, as the bears continued to advance, he let off a shot. A bear-cub of three years old was hit in the leg and fell to the ground. Then the whole army halted, surprised and a little alarmed, and the chiefs called a council to decide what was to be done.

Take courage, bears, there is just one more obstacle to be overcome and then all will be over. Inside the castle there are things to eat and drink and amuse oneself with, and perhaps it is even possible that the city may contain the King's son Tony, the little bear kidnapped by hunters in the mountains. Tomorrow will be a day of battle. Tomorrow evening, victory.

But the castle had high walls, each twenty times higher than any other walls. Hundreds of men-at-arms, armed to the teeth, stood at their posts in niches of the ramparts, the black mouths of cannon gaped from the loopholes, and the Grand Duke, usually very mean, had distributed bottles of wine, brandy and gin to the soldiers to encourage them, a thing which had never occurred in living memory, even on days of national rejoicing.

At six o'clock the following morning trumpeters gave the alarm from every direction. The bears, chanting their national anthem, hurled themselves into the assault. But... but... muskets

64

and sabres against walls of stone and gates of iron? From above there came volleys of fire, flames, smoke, shouting, it was like judgment day. Someone from the top of the fortress was even hurling down boulders.

« Forward, my brave beasts! » cried King Leander, cheering them on to battle. But it was all very well — they were down below, the enemy above. And one by one the bravest of his warriors fell at his side and breathed their last. They were dying like flies, these magnificent mountain bears, and Leander himself did not know if he would ever come out of it alive. Some of them, digging their claws into the crevices, endeavoured to climb up at the corners; one would climb ten feet, another fifteen, and then a bullet would make them fall.

It was an utter disaster.

But if that is so, why is it that in the picture, which certainly corresponds to the truth, we see the bears climbing over the top of the ramparts and some of them even on the chimney tops of the fortress, still higher than the Grand Ducal soldiers? Why does that drawing make it look as if the bears were winning? Why does the artist play this joke on us?

Because a week has gone by in the meantime, that is why; and after being badly defeated in the first attempt the bears had prepared a second assault. An old bear called Marzipan, particularly gifted at mechanics, went to the King and said: « Your Majesty, things are not going well. At the first battle we caught it badly. The same thing will happen at the second, Your Majesty... »

« I know, my dear Marzipan, » replied Leander. « It is very bad, shocking. »

65

« We were completely lacking in common sense, » continued Marzipan who was a blunt, forthright sort of bear, « and we shall be again, unless... »

« Unless what? »

« Unless we can find fifty bears or so who do not suffer from giddiness. Come and see, Your Majesty. I have made a few little things... » And he took him to see.

In a vacant corner the brilliant Marzipan had erected a workshop and fabricated some strange machines out of material picked up here and there during the journey. There was an immense mortar big enough to hold a bull, horns and all, there was a gigantic catapult, there were enormously long ladders and all manner of other devilish contraptions.

« With the help of these, » said Marzipan, after he had explained their use, « you will see how we shall succeed. »

And they did in fact succeed. When the bears returned to the attack the Grand Duke did not even leave his rooms to go and watch, he was so sure that they would be decisively routed. He even changed his uniform and put on a white one embroidered with silver and purple because he intended to go to the theatre that evening. All he did was to order another ration of spirit for the soldiers, to encourage them.

But wine and brandy did not help, for you can see for yourselves what happened.

They light the long fuse and the great cannon roars,
And swift as an arrow a gallant bear soars,
And riding astride on the cannon ball's back
Looks as much at his ease as if riding a hack

66

Led by their King, Leander, the bears lay siege to Cormorant Castle, on the edge of the capital, and conquer it after thirty-two hours of the bitterest fighting, thanks to the wise foresight of the bear Marzipan, and the machines invented by him.

(Such a steed was once used, so the legend avows, on
Another occasion by Baron Münchhausen).

Now see the dreaded catapult,
Another bear within the spoon.
Will the brave creature get a jolt?
Will they not send him off too soon?
Like a great bird he cleaves the sky,
Then down the vaulted heaven he drops,
To land as cool as you or I
Among the fortress' chimney tops.

What of the scaling ladders? Like great spide-
Rs they are ramping up the fortress side.
Some of them bend, some of them snap like straws
Beneath the weight of all those eager paws.
(Pray notice at the bottom on the right
A sad example of this very plight),
And there's a warrior pausing there a minute
To hold his head, which has a bullet in it.
But shortly he will take the field again
And press the siege with all his might and main
Thus proving to the letter
« From good to better. »

Now while the fort commanders are consulting,
Some twenty-seven bears are catapulting,
Twenty-three more are firing off the gun,
And more are climbing ladders one by one.

The Ducal soldiers, dazed and alcoholic,
Unused to these contraptions diabolic,
With too much brandy walzing round their stomachs
Are in a flummox.

Now begins a hurly bur-
Ly, shrieks and yells and « Sauve qui peut ! »
One runs away, one leaps the ramparts
And falls into the ditch's damp parts.
All shout orders contradictory,
Pride has a fall and the bears have a victory.

Meanwhile, in the Grand Theatre Excelsior urbanity, luxury and elegance reigned that evening for the gala performance in honour of the Grand Duke. A week earlier the bears had been driven back from the gates, that was an event well worth celebrating. The room was positively aglitter with precious stones and gorgeous uniforms. There was an Indian prince with his princess, there were officers of all the services in full dress, there were counts, viscounts, marquises, baronets and even a Landgraf, though we are not quite sure what this is; there were two high officials of the Persian court, and there was also Professor Ambrose, incognito (though how was he to remain incognito with a face like that, which one could recognise a hundred yards away?) He was all alone in a box wearing his inseparable top-hat a yard and a half tall.

The programme, specially chosen for the Grand Duke, was as follows:

> The ballet of the sycamore,
> Six dancers and a blackamoor,
> Clowns and Augustes and their followers,
> Fire-eaters, sword-swallowers,

73

Men who chew up packs of cards
With mouths that measure seven yards,
Lions and tigers, harmless beasts,
Conjurors, ventriloquists,
(That is men whose stomach speaks).

Performing horses, mermaids, freaks,
Twenty dancing girls from France,
Sixteen piebald elephants;
Performing fleas will next excite you,
Though they are too well trained to bite you.
And last we have, to top the bill,
None but the bear-cub Bobadil,
Small, it is true, but none the less
Sure of immediate success.
His act will make you lyrical;
Never was such a miracle!

The audience had heard that morning that the bears had returned to the attack on the city, and to tell the truth they were a little uneasy. But the arrival at the theatre of the Grand Duke with the Grand Duchess banished their fears; if their Highnesses deigned to be present at the performance then, thank heaven, it meant that things were going well. And the orchestra played, the ballet girls danced as lightly as butterflies, and the ventriloquist produced from the depths of his innards, to the incredulity of the country bumpkins who were convinced it must be a trick, a voice such as was never heard, not even from the sepulchre.

74

Now and then the Grand Duke made a sign and an official rushed to his side to receive orders.

« What news? » asked the Grand Duke.

« All is well, Your Serene Highness, » replied the official, lacking the courage to tell the truth, which would have been anything but cheerful. And the orchestra continued playing, the ballerinas danced, the conjurers produced live rabbits out of top-hats and the ventriloquist made his stomach speak about all manner of things, and even made it sing a little song which was much applauded. Was not everything going perfectly?

In reality everything was going to rack and ruin, the bears had conquered the fortress and were already overrunning the streets of the capital.

Finally the catastrophe was revealed in the most dramatic manner, in the theatre itself. Amidst the frenzied applause of the crowd, the bear-cub Bobadil had already begun his astonishing feats, walking on a tightrope sixty feet up from the floor of the stage, and twirling a Chinese parasol, when there was a sound of strange voices, a curtain was drawn back, and King Leander in person, followed by a band of armed bears, appeared in the pit.

« Oh heavens, the bears! » shrieked the wife of the Landgraf from a box in the third tier, and, with a sigh, sank down in a swoon.

« Hands up! » said the bears to the elegant assembly. And all of them, frozen with terror, raised their hands (except the ballerinas who were so overcome with fear that they turned into statues with one leg raised in the air, and were later collected

75

just as they were and put up on the façade of the theatre where they can be admired to this day in perpetual memorial of this historical event).

But what is Leander doing? Why, instead of aiming his rifle at his mortal enemy the Grand Duke, does he stare at the bear-cub on the tightrope? Why does he stretch out his paws to the stage, staggering almost as if he were drunk?

> But now that our story is right in the middle,
> What do you say to solving a riddle?
> Whom can you recognise walking the tight-
> Rope? Who knows the acrobat bear-cub by sight?
> Surely you met him and knew him before he
> Came here, and your hair stood on end at his story.
> Think a bit, think a bit, though he has grown, he
> Can surely be none but our little bear...

« Tony! » cried Leander at last in an indescribable voice, as he recognised his kidnapped son.

And the bear-cub, too, recognised the voice of his father, though years had gone by. In fact, in his astonishment he stumbled and nearly fell; but artist as he was, he at once regained his equilibrium and continued the perilous journey, not forgetting to twirl the parasol.

« Papa, papa! » he stammered as he stood suspended among the thousand lights of the theatre, that good little bear whom, from motives of propaganda, they had christened with the ridiculous name of Bobadil.

76

The historic scene in the Grand Theatre Excelsior as the victorious bears force their way in. King Leander recognises the equilibrist as his son kidnapped when small, and the Grand Duke, out of revenge, fires straight at the bear-cub.

But suddenly, BANG! Everybody jumped. The Grand Duke had understood all and, in order to avenge himself, had aimed at Tony with his infallible pistol with its handle of onyx adorned with precious stones! He could have aimed at Leander, his immediate enemy. But no, he was a great deal more wicked than was generally supposed, and he preferred to kill the son.

Horror of horrors! To save time we will refrain from describing the tumult which followed. Everyone shouted, swore and wept. Naturally, the bears in the pit had immediately opened fire, riddling with bullets the Grand Duke, who collapsed, wounded in a thousand places. Through the theatre spread an acrid odour of gunpowder, which the old soldiers sniffed with satisfaction but which made the ladies and damsels cough.

And what of Tony? Alas, Tony was wounded and fell headlong to the stage, right in the midst of the ballerinas who had just been turned to stone. He lay there unconscious, while his father hastened to his aid.

Close in his arms Leander holds his son,
While down his royal face the teardrops run:
« Speak to me, dearest Tony, look around you,
« How can you leave me just when I have found you? »
With all his loving strength he holds him fast,
The bear-cub lifts his heavy lids at last
And answers, « Dearest father, I must die,
« And all that I can do is say Goodbye. »
All hearts can break, even the hearts of kings.
« No, dearest Tony, do not say such things,
« For soon you will forget your grief and pain,

79

« And soon a happy time will come again.
« Swift as a flash will pass these doleful hours,
« And nothing will be left but joy and flowers. »

Joy and flowers! But nobody believes it. With glistening eyes, high dignitaries and important personages bare their heads in silence. Look, even Professor Ambrose's beard is quivering. Is there no hope for the young bear? Has all his father's labour been in vain? Will this tragedy mar the great victory? Can destiny be so cruel?

>One
>>Two
>>>Three
>>>>Four

>These
>>Black
>>>Thoughts
>>>>Soar;

>Fear
>>Sorrow
>>>Doubt
>>>>Despair

>Hover
>>In the
>>>Silent
>>>>Air.

Chapter 7

And while the cub lay in a pool of blood, while King Leander burst into desperate sobbing, while the spectators of this terrible scene remained motionless in their places, overcome with pity and amazement, while a tragic silence reigned in the great theatre, accustomed to singing, music and applause, a white dove flew in through a window which had been left open, and began to flutter joyously about the building.

It was the dove of peace and goodwill, and as many things had come to her knowledge she thought she had arrived just at the right moment to help celebrate the finding of the kidnapped bear-cub. But on glancing about her she saw at once from the faces of all around that something very wrong was happening instead. An instant later she noticed King Leander clasping his wounded son in his arms.

The dove hesitated. Her gay flutterings were inopportune, then. The audience looked at her with evident disapproval. Should she go away again? Or hide in a dark corner? But a happy inspiration led her to alight on the top-hat of Professor Ambrose, who was uneasily present at the tearful scene.

All eyes turned then to the old astrologer. King Leander, too, looked at Ambrose. And Ambrose looked at King Leander.

One thought dominated the whole theatre. Only the wizard, with a stroke of his magic wand, could save the young bear; what made him hesitate?

He hesitated because after the episode of Count Molfetta's wild boars he had only one spell left, and if he used this one too, then farewell wizardry! He would become a poor, ordinary old man again, wretched and ugly into the bargain; and if he got ill he would have to send for the doctor and take disgusting medicines like any other invalid instead of becoming well and bright at one stroke. How could such a sacrifice be expected of him? Many though the accounts were that King Leander had to settle with the wizard, he himself, good-natured beast that he was, had not the courage to demand such a gift, but restricted himself to gazing at Ambrose in silence.

> But now a little sound is heard above
> The silence like a heart-beat; and the dove
> Pecks at the Wizard's hat,
> Pit, pat, pit, pat,
> As if to say « why is your heart so stony?
> « How can you miss this wonderful occasion
> « To save poor Tony?
> « If selfishness would yield to our persuasion
> « You could
> « Do so much good. »

And now of course you will not believe it and you will say that this is just a fairytale and that such things only happen in books, and so on. And yet, at the sight of the little bear dying,

84

Sicily conquered, the gallant legions of bears parade in the market square. The little bear-cub Prince Tony is also able to be present, saved by the intervention of the wizard but still a little weak owing to having lost so much blood. For that reason he is seated on an easy chair.

the astrologer felt a sudden pang of regret for all the wicked things he had done out of hatred for King Leander and his bears (like the episodes of the ghosts and Marmoset the Cat!). He felt something burning in his breast and, perhaps a little out of a desire to make a good effect and become a sort of hero, he drew his famous magic wand from under his great coat — oh, how reluctantly! and began to weave a spell for the last time in his life. He could have wished for mountains of gold, for castles, he could have become a king emperor, he could have destroyed whole armies and battle-fleets, he could have married Indian princesses; he could have had everything in the world had it not been for this sacrifice. Instead:

« Fingo, » he said slowly, emphasising it syllable
« Fingo finkity finxit fy,   [by syllable,
Fabula tabula domine dry,
Briccus braccus purly prit
Fory glory fifferit ».

Then the cub opened both his eyes and rose straight to his feet without a trace of the hole the bullet had made (only he felt a little weak from losing so much blood), while King Leander, mad with joy, began to dance all by himself on the stage. The dove, satisfied at last, began to flutter hither and thither again more gaily than ever. A great shout went up: « Long live Professor Ambrose! »

But the astrologer had already vanished. Slipping out through the stage door he ran home clutching the now worthless magic wand and he himself could not have said whether he was sad or strangely happy.

And now, ladies and gentlemen, it is time to celebrate. Some wanted a grand military review, some wanted a midnight ball. After long discussions they ended by deciding on a military review in the morning and a ball with illuminations in the evening. At the review, the cub Tony, still a little weak, was present seated on an easy chair and wrapped in soft coverlets; he was able to take part in the ball, however, and holding his father's hand, opened the grand cotillion to the strains of a polka. This was possible as during the day he had built up his strength with puddings and beefsteaks.

We first repair
To the market square.
With bugle, fife and kettledrum,
Banneret and pennon, here they come,
The trumpets blare, the martial sound
Wakens the echoes all around.
A banquet next, to assuage our pangs
With sugar, chocolate, meringues,
Marzipan, sugarplums, jam puffs, éclairs
(with cream plain or whipped to taste)
Turkish delight, candy, and flowers of paradise
(A special tropical plant which the natives find
                                    [exceedingly nice).
Tarts, macaroons, buns, brandy-snaps, all show forth,
And so on and so forth.

When evening falls the bears celebrate to the strains of a select orchestra, dancing in the park illuminated by a thousand lights, while the reformed Professor Ambrose, unable to take part owing to his age, contents himself with peeping from a corner.

And tra-la-la and tra-la-lay,
So it goes on the livelong day,
While just as soon as it is dark
Lanterns are lighted in the park.
The orchestra to left and right
Keep it up the livelong night,
While the ancient necromancer
Watches; he is not a dancer.

Here is the dawn
And with a yawn
We discover
All is over.

Chapter 8

Life is like that, alas! when we are growing
We think that we have time enough to spare,
And dawdle. All at once we are aware
That thirteen years have passed without our knowing.

We meet again as if nothing had happened, thirteen years
after the last time we saw one another, and King Leander is
still reigning undisturbed in Sicily because no one has ever had
the courage to challenge him. Men and bears live in perfect
harmony and the days go quietly by; one would think that peace
reigned in everybody's heart and that it would last for ever.
Moreover, thanks to work and study they have made much
progress, many new and beautiful palaces have arisen in the
capital, and they have built more and more complicated machines and magnificent carriages and extraordinary flying kites
of many colours. They even say that Professor Ambrose, though
as old as the dome of the cathedral, has taken up his studies
again and (imagine it, at his age!) made himself a new magic
wand, less powerful than the one used up by the bears but
quite good enough for general purposes; the astrologer hopes
at least to be able to extract a small spell from it to cure himself

if he falls ill, that is, not seriously ill, just not quite the thing.

And yet, if you look into the King's eyes you will see that he is not happy. Too often through the great windows of his palace his gaze returns to the distant mountains rising above the topmost towers of the city. « Were the days spent up there not happier ones, » he thinks to himself in secret, « among the solemn solitude of the crags? »

> Then, in those far-off days upon the mountain
> We fed on berries, slept on beds of pine,
> We quenched our thirst at some untrodden fountain.
> Now in Venetian glass we drink our wine.
> "Pâté de foie-gras" is our staple diet,
> At night we sleep beneath an eiderdown.
> How badly off we used to be! How quiet
> And easy life is now! How rich my crown!
> How happy we should be! Why, why regret
> The half-forgotten things we left behind?
> Rocks, torrents, tempests, ice and snow and yet
> A tranquil mind!

Moreover it displeased Leander to see the bears changing under his very eyes. Once modest, simple, patient and easygoing, they were now proud, ambitious and full of capricious fancies. Not in vain had they lived thirteen years among men.

It displeased Leander especially to see that instead of contenting themselves, as formerly, with their own beautiful fur, the majority of his bears now wore clothes, uniforms and coats copied from men, thinking they looked elegant; and it never

96

occurred to them that they were making themselves look ridiculous. At the risk of heat-stroke some of them were even seen walking about wearing thick fur coats, to show the world that they were not short of money.

But that was not the worst! They went to law on the slightest pretext, they used bad language, they got up late in the morning, they smoked cigars and pipes, they grew fat, and day by day they became uglier. Nevertheless the King kept his patience, restricted himself to a kindly scolding now and then and preferred on the whole to turn a blind eye.

After all, these crimes were not very great. But how long could things go on in this way? Where would it lead? King Leander was uneasy, he had a vague feeling that some evil was impending.

And sure enough some strange things began to happen.
The first mysterious occurrence was

The Theft of Professor Ambrose's New Magic Wand.

The wizard had already finished preparing it with all the necessary materials, and was just giving it the finishing touches when it was suddenly stolen from him. They looked here, they looked there, but found nothing. There was a police enquiry; no result. So then the wizard went to King Leander to tell him what had happened.

Leander could not get over it. Such a serious theft had never occurred during his reign.

97

He took counsel with his Grand Chamberlain, Saltpetre (a very intelligent bear whose weakness it was, however, to think himself very handsome and to wear a long feather on his hat), and they decided to convene the whole human population to whom, from the balcony of his palace, the King addressed the following speech:

« Ladies and gentlemen, » he said, « some evilly disposed person has robbed our worthy Professor Ambrose of a magic wand which he has recently made. »

« Citizens, » he continued, « this is a disgrace! Will the person who stole it please raise his hand? »

But no hand was raised.

« Very well, » said Leander, « it is possible that the culprit is not present. But I will say one thing; if within ten days the thief is not discovered in one way or another, I shall hold you all responsible and you will each pay the astrologer a thousand ducats. »

« Ooooh! » murmured the crowd, alarmed. One person even threw a stone at the King.

« What? » replied the King, feeling his rage mounting. « Very well then, two thousand ducats each. And mind you behave! »

This said, he returned to his apartments, while men and women dispersed with the most varied comments.

Then the astrologer came to the palace and said:

« Your Majesty, you have convened the humans, and I thank you for it. But why did you not speak to the bears too? »

« To the bears? What do you mean? »

« I mean that though my wand may have been stolen by a man, it may also have been stolen by a bear. »

98

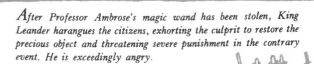

After Professor Ambrose's magic wand has been stolen, King Leander harangues the citizens, exhorting the culprit to restore the precious object and threatening severe punishment in the contrary event. He is exceedingly angry.

« By a bear? » exclaimed Leander, thunderstruck. Since when had his bears been guilty of such things?

« Yes, Sire, by a bear, » repeated the astrologer, nettled. « Do you think bears so much better than men? »

« I should hope so! Why, bears do not even know the meaning of the word "theft". »

« Ha, ha! » sneered the wizard.

« Did you sneer, Professor? »

« Yes, Sire, I sneered, » replied Ambrose. « I could tell you some fine stories, if I liked, about your sweet, innocent animals. »

Compose yourselves, children, and hark
To the mystery of Artichoke Park.

Chapter 9

The second mystery, in fact, was

The Secret of Artichoke Park.

« One evening, » said the Professor, « as I was going for a stroll in Artichoke Park... »

« Where my Chamberlain, Saltpetre, lives? » interrupted King Leander.

« I know nothing of that, » said the wizard, « I only know that while I was wandering through the shrubbery I suddenly raised my eyes above the tree-tops, and you will never guess what I saw ! »

« A bird? » suggested Leander, devoured with curiosity, « or a monster, perhaps? »

« I saw a palace, all of marble, illuminated in every window and gleaming in the night. Pricked by curiosity, I approached. Music and laughter sounded from the windows as if a great feast were in progress. Then at ground level I noticed other illuminated openings. I bent down to inspect. And there I saw an immense cellar, bigger than a church, and along the walls there were Titanic barrels from which wine was streaming in floods. And laden tables, and bottles of liquor everywhere, and musicians playing, and servants coming and going, bearing monumental puddings; and seated at table... »

« Who? Who? » interrupted Leander again.

« Your bears, Your Majesty, your bears! Drunk as lords, every one of them, and bawling out improper songs! Some dressed in rich cloaks, some in evening dress, some broaching the barrels so as to let the wine pour straight down their throats, some unconscious under the table! »

« It is a slander! » panted King Leander.

« I saw it with my own eyes, I swear I did! » protested the wizard.

« Very well, then I shall go and see for myself at once. »

The King wasted no time. Night had already fallen. Accompanied by a bodyguard, he went to Artichoke Park, and there, above the heavy darkness of the trees, he beheld the gleaming domes of a fantastic palace, with lights twinkling like stars. Foaming with rage he advanced, hoping to catch the drunkards red-handed. But when he emerged from the thick wood and reached the road, the marvellous palace had vanished. In its place was a wretched hut with one small lighted window. The King went closer.

He burst open the door and found his Chamberlain, Saltpetre, reading a large book by the light of an oil lamp.

« What are you doing here at this hour, Saltpetre? »

« I am studying the laws of the Constitution, Your Majesty, and this is my modest abode. »

But Leander was sniffing about the room. There was such a curious smell in the air... strange, one would have said a smell

106

New symptoms of corruption among the bears. Ambrose says that in the cellars of a mysterious castle he discovered animals abandoning themselves to shameful orgies. The account leaves King Leander perplexed and much disgusted.

of flowers, food and good wine. The King began to have his suspicions.

But what could he say then and there? « Goodnight, Saltpetre, » he stammered. « I came your way by chance, you know, so I dropped in to pay you a little visit. » And he went out, somewhat embarrassed, and returned to his palace meditating on the enigma.

All that night he could not sleep. Tormenting doubts presented themselves stormily to his mind.

Had the wizard lied?

But if so, how had he, Leander, also seen the palace beyond the trees?

But then how had the palace managed to vanish so suddenly?

Was it an enchanted palace?

But who could work spells except the wizard?

But had not the wizard's magic wand been stolen?

Then who would work such magic except the thief?

And what was Saltpetre doing in that solitary hut? And how explain that strange smell of roast meat and wine?

Was Saltpetre implicated in this wretched affair?

But Leander's indignation reached its peak at dawn when they came to announce the third mysterious event to him, namely :

The Robbery of the Great Universal Bank.

Armed and masked bandits had assaulted the palace by night, killed the sentries, forced the iron doors and made off with the whole treasure. The State treasury no longer possessed a farthing.

And the culprits? Saltpetre demonstrated with very convincing arguments that they could have been no ordinary criminals. They were certainly criminals guided by a cunning man who must be versed in mechanics and knowledgeable in science. One man only, according to Saltpetre, could have organised such an affair. And his name was Ambrose.

It seemed to Leander then as if a veil had fallen from his eyes; why had he not realised it sooner? Why had he not thought of it for himself? But now all was explained; Ambrose was jealous of the bears on whom he had spent his two spells, Ambrose had pretended that his magic wand had been stolen, in order to prevent the King asking further favours of him and in order to bring discredit on the animals. Ambrose, still in order to slander the bears, had invented the story of the nocturnal banquet in the cellar (and if he, Leander, had thought for an instant that he too had seen the palace, that had been due to autosuggestion). Finally, Ambrose, avid of power and wealth, had organised the bank robbery!

Ambrose was arrested half an hour later, at the express command of the King; and his protests were in vain. They loaded him with chains and locked him up in the deepest and darkest dungeon.

But meanwhile, let us see a minute, what is a certain bear called Dandelion doing, looking all round the bank, among the comings and goings of the policemen charged with the enquiry, and straying about the town with such a foolish air that people think he cannot be quite right in the head?

« Off you go, quick march! » the sentinels shout at him.

But instead, he remains. He puts on a ridiculous expression

110

Who was it who attacked the Grand Universal Bank one night and stole the treasure? Saltpetre the Chamberlain insinuates that the deed was carried out by humans at the instigation of the wizard. But it is possible that this is not exactly what happened.

as if he has not understood, and meanwhile he contrives to peer around, especially where the traces of the thieves are most evident, that is, in front of the iron doors of the treasure chamber which are lying on the ground torn off their hinges.

« Was it Ambrose? » Dandelion asks himself incredulously, and he bends down to pick up from the ground six or seven hairs which have escaped the eye of the municipal police. He sniffs them and looks at them against the light.

« Put that down, Paul Pry! » shouts a man on duty to him. « What was that you just picked up? »

« Nothing, only some hairs. »

« Hairs? Let me see at once, » and the detective had barely seen them before he began to roar like a madman: « Hairs from the beard of the wizard! Inspector! Inspector! Here is the final proof. »

Yet Dandelion still laughs his vacant laugh. They have nothing to do with a beard, nothing to do with the wizard! He has recognised them at once; they are bears' hairs, he would stake his life on it.

Alas! Is it the bears after all who have committed this crime? Then Ambrose is innocent. But now, how to put King Leander on his guard? How to persuade him? How to save Ambrose from the gallows? Dandelion is one of those bears who always keep their eyes open. He knows many things besides this business of the treasure, of which King Leander has no notion. And now there is not a moment to lose. At the risk of giving him a rude shock, the King must be warned. Dandelion decides to send him a letter.

Chapter 10

So, by first post next morning King Leander received the following note which we transcribe word for word with all its spelling mistakes (for at school Dandelion had always been something of a blockhead).

« Dear King, You have a frend you should not trust,
And now he wants you to comit injust-
Ice, for an inocent is being locked up
And so of course the theef is verry bucked up.
You say "why don't you give the name you've writen of?"
And I reply "My head might well get biten off!"
But some fine evening shortly when you have a new
Suit on, go down to 5 Acacia Avenue,
And you'll be grateful you were sent to spy on
Such doings, Yours sinserely,

DANDELION. »

What fresh devilment was this? A new mystery? Were there not enough already? The King hardly knew where to turn. But he had always liked Dandelion and he decided to follow

117

his advice. When it was night he put on evening dress for the first time in his life (for he detested clothes of any sort) and went entirely alone to the place indicated. The streets were all deserted.

No. 5 Acacia Avenue was an elegant villa. The King knocked, the door was opened, a liveried major-domo conducted him up a flight of stairs, and at the top of the stairs, wonder of wonders! there was a great hall. There Leander, paralysed with amazement, saw scores of highly elegant bears — some even wearing monocles — playing at cards and gambling. A hubbub of voices was heard. « Well played! Capot! » cried one. « Ten thousand, no, twenty thousand to me! » And another cried: « Curses on it, they have broken the bank! I am ruined! Brutes! » Piles of gold changed hands in these capricious games of chance, passing from one to another with extraordinary rapidity. Here and there quarrels broke out. Depravity and disgrace! But the King's blood froze in his veins when his gaze reached the end of the hall. Do you know what he saw? Tony, his son, squandering his princely revenues and already down to his last few pennies. Seated with him at the table were three sinister bears who looked real ruffians. One of them said: « Hurry up, young man, you still owe me five hundred ducats, » and he said it in such a way that Tony, frightened and without a penny in his pocket, took from his neck a precious gold chain given him by his father on his twenty-first birthday and threw it down on the green cloth.

« Villain! » cried the King at this point from the doorway, and he dashed across the hall, seized his young son by the collar, paying no attention to the protests of the gamblers, who did

118

At the suggestion of Dandelion, the detective bear, King Leander visits a villa in Acacia Avenue and discovers a gambling den. Worse than that, he discovers his son Tony, who is squandering all he possesses on this ruinous vice.

not recognise him, dragged him first to the exit and then, without saying a word, back to the palace. Little Tony, humiliated, was sobbing.

And now for energetic measures. The very next morning, the shameful gambling house was raided by the police, but only the staff were there and nobody knew who the proprietor was. The house had three storeys:

Ground floor:

Roulette room, bar and cloakroom.

First floor:

Large room for card-playing and strong room where the mysterious proprietor amassed his gains.

Second floor:

Kitchen and banquet hall.

Third and last storey:

Pantry, servants' hall with bowling alley and room of correction where gamblers detected cheating were first beaten with rods and then obliged to learn improving poetry by heart such as "The Grasshopper and the Ant" (this was because the establishment, with great hypocrisy, took pains to make it appear that the house was frequented by bears only for their own good).

All this staggered King Leander. So the arrest of the wizard had not been enough to stop the rot. Who was really the proprietor of this gambling house? And why had Dandelion not had the courage to explain himself more clearly? The more the King thought about it, the more confused his ideas became. But he always returned to one conclusion; someone, who was not Professor Ambrose, was sowing crime and corruption among the bears. There must be someone rich, powerful and very cunning at work behind the scenes, taking good care not to be discovered. If they did not unmask him forthwith, farewell peace and tranquillity!

Then King Leander, in order to take counsel and explore the ground, ordered a general assembly. Men and bears, leaving their games or their business, met together in the square, where the following dialogue took place:

THE KING, in tragic tones:
Respond! Which of you stole the magic wand?

THE MEN in chorus:
No, not we!

THE BEARS, idem:
Nor me, nor me!

THE KING:
Saltpetre, can you guess
Who started all this wickedness?

SALTPETRE:
I wonder, Sire, to see you waste a thought
Upon such trifles. It is really nought.

THE KING:
And I suppose you think we wove a spell
To steal the treasure from the bank as well?

SALTPETRE:
Enough, enough, Sire, kindly disabuse
Your mind of such sad thoughts. I bring good news.

122

THE KING:
First let me finish, you can tell me then.
Who is the owner of that gambling den?

THE MEN in chorus:
O King, 'twere best to let things be,
It could but bring you misery.

SALTPETRE (holding up a sheet of paper):
I wonder how this monument will strike you,
Is it not like you?

It was a drawing of an immense statue representing King Leander himself; and as even bears have their share of vanity, all the King's worries vanished in a trice. « Oh, my worthy Saltpetre! » he cried, much moved, « it is only now, that I realise how fond you are of me. To think that I ever doubted it, even for a moment! » And he at once forgot all the disasters.

This time — and I am sorry to have to admit it, but it is true — King Leander really behaved like a great simpleton. The thought of the monument made him lose his head completely. His other preoccupations vanished as if by magic. Who cared about Ambrose? Who cared about the crimes? Who cared about the gambling den? Leander at once sent a battalion of bears to quarry marble from the mountains, engaged engineers, masons and stone-cutters and ordered work to be started.

In a short time the immense statue began to rise upward stone by stone, on the top of a hill commanding the city. From there it could be seen scores of miles away. Hundreds of bears laboured at it day and night, and every so often the King visited the site, where the chamberlain explained everything to him. Very soon, stone by stone they reached the head. The muzzle of a gigantic bear began to appear against the blue skyline. Engineers flew over the city in balloons or small dirigibles to judge of the effect.

« But why is the muzzle so long? » thought Leander. « My muzzle is nothing like as long as that. One would really think it was Saltpetre, seen from a distance. »

However, he had not the courage to say so openly, in order not to hurt anybody's feelings. The majestic statue towered over the city, the bay and the distant sea, and in three days it was to be unveiled.

But as it is decreed that there is never to be any peace in life, a little group of fishermen came running into the market-place in the grip of terror: « Help! help! » they cried. « The end of the world is coming! »

They related that an immense sea-serpent had appeared, who, rearing his gigantic head and neck from the waves, had swooped down on the shore and already devoured three houses and a church, including the parish priest and the sacristan.

To pacify his King's wrath, Saltpetre the Chamberlain causes a gigantic monument to be erected in his honour. But joy is short-lived. Down there on the right various terrified fishermen are coming running, and they are certainly bringing bad news.

Chapter 11

MEN: Monster of the deep
From the world outside
What do you betide,
Joy or tears to weep?

THE SERPENT: No, my fatal hiss
Speaks of tenebrose
Mysteries none knows
From the black abyss.

MEN: From the black abyss
Jesus crucified,
Who for our sake died,
Will bring us all to bliss.

THE SERPENT: Hear the passing bell,
Death and doom are yours
In the venomed jaws
Of the gates of hell!

MEN: Fiery pestilence
      O'er the kingdom runs.
      Fly, you mothers, hence!
      Save your little ones!

Then all the mothers ran out of their houses on the shore carrying their children in their arms; and men too took flight, and so did dogs, and so did birds who could really fly! But to save the city King Leander went down to the sea with his bravest bears and boarded a bark to fight the monster. He himself was armed with a powerful harpoon, the others with firearms and arquebuses. Saltpetre was there too, with a large rifle; although the King had told him he might stay at home he had absolutely insisted on coming too. While an immense crowd gathered on the shore watching with baited breath, the little ship, vigorously propelled by the oarsmen, left the shore and approached the terrible serpent which alternately raised and lowered its head among the foaming waves.

Leander, standing right on the bow, lifted his harpoon, ready to strike the first blow.

And behold, there rose from the waves a great round neck as thick as a treetrunk, ending in the most terrifying head it is possible to imagine. The serpent opened his mouth like an enormous cavern and threw himself upon the fragile bark. Then Leander hurled the harpoon.

Whistling through the air, the shaft went swift as lightning and buried itself in the monster's throat at least three spans deep. A loud detonation followed; the King's companions had fired simultaneously, to give the final blow.

130

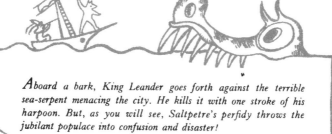

Aboard a bark, King Leander goes forth against the terrible sea-serpent menacing the city. He kills it with one stroke of his harpoon. But, as you will see, Saltpetre's perfidy throws the jubilant populace into confusion and disaster!

For a moment the bark was hidden in a dense cloud of smoke from the firing. Then, while the sea-serpent sank in a fountain of blood and a tremendous shout of joy echoed from shore to shore, the wind blew the smoke away. And then they saw.

In the bow of the little vessel King Leander lay on his back, a rivulet of blood trickling from between his shoulderblades. At the same time one of the oarsmen threw down his oar, jumped to his feet brandishing an axe, sprang towards the Chamberlain, Saltpetre, and with a single stroke severed the head from his body. It was the bear Dandelion.

Tragedy!

Having embarked specially so as to keep an eye on Saltpetre, the gallant detective bear had seen all; profiting by the general confusion, the Chamberlain had fired not at the monster but at his King. Alas! the timid Dandelion had suspected the truth for some time, but had not had the courage to tell his sovereign so, namely, that it was Saltpetre who had stolen the magic wand, Saltpetre who was responsible for the banquets in the cellar of the enchanted castle, Saltpetre who had robbed the bank, Salt-petre who had organised the gambling den, Saltpetre who had plotted to destroy Leander and usurp his crown. Even the statue had been meant for him, Saltpetre, and not for the King, who had never had such a long muzzle. But Dandelion, always hoping that the Chamberlain would betray himself of his own accord, had contented himself with telling Leander about the affair of the gambling den. And now it was too late.

With the King on board, mortally wounded, the little ship returned to the shore amid a profound silence, for the crowd, stricken dumb with sorrow, could not even weep.

133

On disembarking, Leander was taken to the palace; doctors hastened to his aid but they did not dare to speak. A few, however, shook their heads, as if to say that there was no hope.

Chapter 12

And now twilight had fallen, and King Leander had sent for his son and his most faithful bears, for he felt that he was about to die. Through the little hole made by the bullet life was ebbing drop by drop.

In order not to give him further cause for grief, no one had had the heart to tell him that the magic wand and the gold taken from the bank had been found actually in Saltpetre's palace, that that magnificent palace did in fact exist and that on that famous evening, realising the King was approaching, Saltpetre had made it vanish temporarily by a stroke of the magic wand which he had stolen.

But the sovereign was very pleased to see Professor Ambrose enter the room, after his release from prison.

« Do not leave us, papa, » implored his young son Tony. « What shall we do without you? You led us down from the mountains, you freed us from our enemies and from the seaserpent. Who will command our people now? ».

« Do not grieve, dearest Tony, » murmured his father. « No one is indispensable in this world. When I am gone there will be some other brave bear to wear the crown. But for your own salvation, my brothers, you must promise me one thing. »

« Speak, O King, » they said, falling on one knee. « We are listening. »

137

« Go back to the mountains, » said Leander slowly. « Leave this city, where you have found riches but not peace of mind. Take off those ridiculous human clothes. Throw away your gold. Abandon your cannon, your rifles, and all the other devilish contraptions that men have shown you. Return to what you were before. How happily we used to live in those solitary caverns open to the winds, how different it was from these hateful palaces full of vanity and corruption! Forest plants and wild honey will still seem the most exquisite food to you. Oh, drink pure spring water again, and not wine which ruins your health. It will be hard to part with so many beautiful things, I know, but you will be the happier for it afterwards, and you will look the better for it. We have changed, my friends, that is the truth, we are not what we were. »

« Oh, forgive us, good King, » they said. « You will see that we shall obey you. »

Then King Leander raised himself on his pillows to breathe in the fragrant evening air. Night was falling. From the open windows one could see the city shining marvellously in the last rays of the sun, the gardens all in bloom, and, in the distance, a line of blue sea.

There was a long silence. Then suddenly the birds began to sing. They flew in at the window, each holding a little flower in its beak and, fluttering gently, let it fall on the bed of the dying bear.

« Goodbye, little Tony, » the King whispered once more. « Now I must really leave you. I beg you, if it would not be too much trouble, to carry me up to the mountains too. Farewell, my friends, farewell, my beloved people. Farewell to you

In accordance with the last wishes of their valiant and unfortunate King, the bears forsake riches, elegance and debauchery, to return to their ancient mountains. They depart in an endless column. We shall never see them again. Farewell, farewell!

too, Ambrose, a little stroke of your magic wand might perhaps help my worthy beasts come to their senses again! »

He closed his eyes. It seemed to him that kindly shades, the spirits of bears of old, his ancestors, his father, and comrades fallen in battle, drew near to him to accompany him to the far-off paradise for bears, the land of eternal spring. And he ended his life with a smile.

The next day the bears left. To the amazement of men (and also to their regret, for on the whole the beasts had been liked), they left their palaces and possessions as they were, without taking so much as a pin with them, they piled up their arms, their decorations, their banners, their uniforms and so on, in one of the squares, and set fire to them. They gave all their money to the poor, down to the very last farthing. And in silence they filed along the road down which they had come thirteen years earlier from victory to victory.

They say that the crowd of humans lining the walls of the city broke into sobs and laments when the body of King Leander, borne on the shoulders of four mighty bears, emerged from the main gateway, surrounded by a multitude of torches and flags; and perhaps you, too, will be a little sorry to see him depart for ever.

THE CHILDREN:
> Dearest bear-cubs, do not go,
> Dark the night and strange the way.
> Wicked fairies wait to throw
> Terrors in your path till day.

141

Just a little longer stay,
And we promise not to tease you,
We would find new games to play
And do everything to please you.

We would give you sweets to eat,
Sweets our fathers brought from Spain;
We would think of some new treat,
We would lend you our new train,

And our scooter and our kite
And our bricks, and all we could.
We would sing with you at night.
If you stay, we WILL be good.

THE BEAR-CUBS:
Dearest children, cry no more,
Do not say such things to us,
For this voyage mysterious
Made us sad enough before.

How we wish that we could stay
With you on the grassy plain
We shall never see again;
How we hate to go away!

But go we must. Our Destiny
Calls to the mountain-tops anew,
And like a dream our history
Is ended now. Adieu, adieu!

And so, along the white road stretching away to the mountains, the immense procession receded, until the very last squadron had left the city, looking back to salute.

Slowly, slowly the lengthy ranks appeared smaller and more slender. Towards sunset nothing could be seen save a thin, black streak on the brow of a distant hill. (Further away still, at an incalculable distance, the towering peaks glittered, midst ice and solitude). Then nothing more was visible.

Where did they bury King Leander? In what pinewood, in what green pasture, in the heart of what rock? No one has ever known, probably no one ever will know. And what did the bears do afterwards, in their ancient kingdom? Those are secrets guarded for all eternity by the mountains. In memory of the bears there remains only the uncompleted monument, its head half finished, dominating the roofs of the capital. But tempests, gales and the centuries have little by little destroyed even this. Last year only a few stones remained, crumbling and unrecognisable, piled up in the corner of a garden.

« What are those strange boulders? » we asked an aged inhabitant who was passing by.

« Why, don't you know, Sir? » he said pleasantly. « They are the remains of an antique statue. Do you see? Once upon a time... » And he began to tell the story.

THE END

Index of Illustrations

146

A READER'S COMPANION TO

The
Bears' Famous
Invasion *of* Sicily

by Lemony Snicket

Now that you have finished Dino Buzzati's *The Bears' Famous Invasion of Sicily,* you are probably sighing with the satisfaction of completing a good story, or wiping one last tear from your eye as you contemplate the melancholy ending, or holding your empty glass upside down over your mouth in the hopes that there is one or two more drops of your Buzzati Cocktail left inside for you to enjoy, or doing all three of these things at once, or getting up from your bed and making sure all the doors and windows are locked in case the werewolf from the list of characters, who does not appear in the story after all, has decided to appear in your neighborhood on this very evening and is attracted to the glow of your bedside lamp as he wanders the sidewalks in search of nourishment. In any case, you are probably in no mood to read any sort of reader's guide hidden in the back of a book.

149

In all likelihood these pages are entirely useless. In all likelihood, you have read Dino Buzzati's *The Bears' Famous Invasion of Sicily* as an assignment in the school or headquarters where you spend most of your days. In all likelihood, your instructor has helped you explore the valuable information contained in Mr. Buzzati's history. In all likelihood, you have reached a thorough appreciation of the philosophical truths of *The Bears' Famous Invasion of Sicily,* even if you are not a bear, or have no interest in invading Sicily. In all likelihood—a phrase which here means "probably," although it is such a rare expression that it is unusual to find it more than four times in a single paragraph—you can safely ignore this last section of the book, just as you can safely ignore that suspicious shadow that has just appeared across your window shade, because in all likelihood it is not a werewolf.

However, there is a slim possibility that the instructors at your school or headquarters are a bit foolish, and instead of assigning a valuable work such as *The Bears' Famous Invasion of Sicily,* they have chosen to focus on something less important, such as long division, or planting bean sprouts in cups, or learning how to be a good sport. I cannot imagine an instructor who would do such a foolish thing,

150

but if this is the case, you have probably read Dino Buzzati's book on your own, and you may want to serve as your own instructor and learn as much as you can from *The Bears' Famous Invasion of Sicily* before it is too late. In that case, you may find this guide helpful.

The Reader's Companion is divided into sections—one for each of the sections of the book. As you read the companion, you may want to go back to each section to refresh your memory, keeping one finger here in the guide so you do not lose your place. I recommend using your own finger, as you never know where the fingers of others have been.

SECTION ONE

Once upon a time . . .
Page 9

A brief summary of events: Mr. Buzzati writes a brief description of something that happens before the story begins: the kidnapping of Tony, son of Leander, by two hunters. In a way, it is this tragic incident that is the cause of all the bears' troubles in Sicily, and so this incident, which happens before the story begins and appears before the book begins, is actually the beginning of the story as well as the beginning of the book.

The lesson of this brief section is clear: Kidnapping, no matter how exciting it is, rarely leads to good things.

QUESTIONS YOU MAY FIND INTERESTING:

- Is hunting a moral act, a phrase which here means "something that is not as wicked as kidnapping, but perhaps a little wicked nonetheless"?
- Why wasn't Tony held for ransom?
- In the illustration, how are the hunters able to stay on the mountain? It looks very steep.

153

SUGGESTED ACTIVITY:

Either by reading a newspaper or by eavesdropping, learn about a recent kidnapping and rescue the kidnapping victim yourself. When my instructor first suggested this activity, I thought she was talking nonsense, but four years later, as I untied her and led her out of the cave hidden behind a very large magazine stand, I realized this was a valuable activity indeed.

SECTION TWO

List of Characters
Page 11

A brief summary of events: In this section of the book, Mr. Buzzati provides a list of the heroes, villains, friends, enemies, monsters, and other mysterious individuals who may or may not appear in the book. Several characters are so distressing that one is tempted to shut the book immediately and forget the whole thing.

The lesson of this section is clear: It is helpful to have a list before embarking on an adventure, so you know who to avoid and who to befriend.

QUESTIONS YOU MAY FIND INTERESTING:

- Which character seems the most interesting, based on this list? Which character seems the most frightening? Which character seems the happiest? The saddest? The tallest? The nastiest? The most likely to enjoy freshly squeezed juice? The most likely to say that he or she will attend a birthday

155

party, but then call and cancel at the last moment?
- Do monsters make a story more interesting, or are they too frightening and ought to be removed from all stories, by force if necessary?
- Do you suppose any of these monsters live in your neighborhood? If so, oh dear. If not, remember they may visit your neighborhood even if they do not live there.
- What was that noise?
- Why are so many of the characters facing to the right?

SUGGESTED ACTIVITY:

Make a list of the heroes, villains, friends, enemies, monsters, and other mysterious individuals in your own life. You will probably have to change this list very often.

SECTION THREE

The Scene

Page 17

A brief summary of events: Mr. Buzzati describes some of the locations in which the story takes place. Some people may find this section slightly boring, but if you don't pay close attention you find yourself lost in the desolate and snowy surroundings of the book.

The lesson of this brief section is clear: If you do not know where you are, it is impossible to conduct a famous invasion.

QUESTIONS YOU MAY FIND INTERESTING:

- Where are you?
- Are you sure?
- Mr. Buzzati describes "palaces of yellow marble" in the city. Do you think yellow is an appropriate color for royal decorating? If not, make another suggestion.
- If you look at a map, you will see that the country of Italy is shaped like a boot, and that

157

the island of Sicily appears to be something that Italy is kicking. What do you think Sicily has done to annoy Italy?

SUGGESTED ACTIVITY:

Draw a map of the various locations in this book, or of other locations you find interesting. Hide the map where it may come in handy. I once found a map left for me by a person I will call Q. Thanks to Q's map, I was able to cross the Grim River without passing through the lair of a notoriously ill-tempered trout.

SECTION FOUR

Chapter *1*
Page 19

A brief summary of events: King Leander leads the bears down from the mountains to the plains, where they might find food and (Leander secretly hopes) his lost son, Tony. Immediately, the bears find themselves in battle with the forces of the Grand Duke, but the bears emerge victorious, thanks to the snow-building skills of the bear Titan.

The lesson of this chapter is clear: All sorts of terrible things happen when there isn't enough food to go around.

QUESTIONS YOU MAY FIND INTERESTING:

- Is it fair for the bears to come down to where humans live, looking for food? Is it fair for the Duke's soldiers to shoot at them? Is it fair for the bears to crush them with giant snowballs?
- Often, if you point out something that isn't fair, someone will reply, "Life isn't fair." What is to be done with such people?

159

SUGGESTED ACTIVITY:

In a horrifying passage, Mr. Buzzati writes that the Duke's soldiers "killed without mercy every living thing they encountered up there, old woodcutters, shepherd boys, squirrels, marmots, and even innocent little birds. Only the bears escaped." This means, sadly, that only the history of the bears has survived after all these years. See if you can discover, through careful research or from writing one yourself, the history of old woodcutters, shepherd boys, squirrels, marmots, or even innocent little birds. If you are not interested in these creatures, consider writing a history of firefighters, because I fear I will not have time to do this myself.

SECTION FIVE

Chapter 2

Page 29

A brief summary of events: Professor Ambrose offers his services to the bears—just in time to use up one of his spells defeating Count Molfetta's army of boars. Please note that it is an army of "boars," a phrase which here means "wild pigs," and not "bores," a phrase which here means "people who tell boring stories." Even the strongest magic spells usually cannot defeat an army of bores.

The lesson of this chapter is clear: If you are being attacked by wild boars, it is useful to have some sort of wizard handy.

QUESTIONS YOU MAY FIND INTERESTING:

- When the boars arrive, King Leander and Professor Ambrose have completely different reactions. The King draws his sword and cries, "Let us die like gallant soldiers!" The Professor begs, "And what about me? What about me?" Which reaction do you admire more? Keep in

161

mind that the Professor ends up saving everyone's life.
- Count Molfetta is a cousin of the Grand Duke, and trains an army of vicious animals to attack anyone the Duke finds repulsive. Do you have any cousins who would do such a thing for you? If you aren't sure, call up your cousins and ask them. Listen for snorting in the background.
- What do you think happened to the boars after they floated away? Balloons eventually pop.

SUGGESTED ACTIVITY:

Before the boars arrive, King Leander and Professor Ambrose argue all night long in profound philosophical conflict, a phrase which here means "without convincing each other that they are right." Tonight, find someone with whom you do not agree, and argue with them until the sun rises.

My my, you must be tired.

Chapter 3

Page 39

A brief summary of events: Professor Ambrose leads the bears to Demon Castle, where they encounter a number of their deceased companions. Together, they throw a wild party, which lasts until three in the morning, when the ghosts vanish—just as they were about to tell King Leander the location of his son.

The lesson of this chapter is clear: Late at night is an excellent time for a party but a bad time to seek important information.

QUESTIONS YOU MAY FIND INTERESTING:

- According to Mr. Buzzati, "There are some mothers who say: 'I cannot imagine what pleasure people get out of telling children ghost stories: it terrifies them, and afterwards at night they start screaming if they hear a mouse.'" Is your mother such a woman? I'm sorry to hear that.

- In the illustration, do you think the figure hovering over the fire is a pair of ghosts with their arms around each other, or the ghost of a pair of Siamese twins?

SUGGESTED ACTIVITY:

Mr. Buzzati claims that ghosts are "natural and innocent things." Other people claim that ghosts are terrifying and violent. Still others claim that ghosts are merely figments of the imagination, and some people don't believe in ghosts during the daytime but aren't quite sure at night. Conduct a ghostly investigation of your own in a nearby castle, cemetery, schoolyard, or dark closet, and see if you can find out for sure. (I failed this part of the reader's guide when I was in school by hiding underneath my covers and whimpering until my instructor changed the subject.)

SECTION SEVEN

Chapter 4

Page 51

A brief summary of events: Leander leads the bears to Three Peak to search for Tony, but the local ogre sets his horrifying pet, Marmoset the Cat, upon the army. All seems lost until the bear Merlin kills the cat with an ingenious digestive strategy, but even so, Tony is not to be found, so all the suffering is for nothing—not only the bears' suffering, but the suffering of the readers who shudder through the entire chapter for no good reason.

The lesson of this chapter is clear: Cats—and their owners—are not to be trusted.

QUESTIONS YOU MAY FIND INTERESTING:

- The bear Merlin saves the day by leaping into the cat's mouth in a brave act of self-sacrifice. Do you think you could sacrifice yourself in this way? Me neither.
- Of course, it turns out that Merlin survives after all. Does this change your mind? Me neither.

165

- In the rhyming section of the chapter, Mr. Buzzati states that Marmoset eats "James Johnses Adolfs Alphonses" and "Normans Nathaniels Davids Daniels." It seems, then, that the beast prefers boys to girls. Why might this be so?

SUGGESTED ACTIVITY:

According to Mr. Buzzati, the ogre catches Marmoset the Cat with a net made of witches' hair. Build such a net yourself, and see if it can truly catch an enormous and ravenous beast. If this task seems too daunting—a word which here means "quite impossible"—make a net out of a piece of tissue paper, and see if it can catch a small, harmless bug.

SECTION EIGHT

Chapter 5

Page 61

A brief summary of events: Faced with yet another obstacle in their quest for food, the bears engage in battle once more with the forces of the Grand Duke, this time at Cormorant Castle. It is a catastrophic failure. A week later they try again, and thanks to the remarkable mechanical mind of the bear Marzipan, the bears carry the day, a phrase which here means "win the battle, although all this bloodshed continues to be quite heartbreaking."

The lesson of this chapter is clear: Sometimes the world appears to be nothing more than a parade of violence and hatred, looming over every living creature like an enormous black shadow. Of course, other times the world seems fine.

QUESTIONS YOU MAY FIND INTERESTING:

- It is almost impossible to find an interesting story—a true story or an imaginary story—that does not contain violence. Why is that?

167

- Would the world, like a story, be less interesting if it did not contain violence?
- These are very troubling things to think about. Let's skip the rest of the questions.

SUGGESTED ACTIVITY:

After such a horrifying chapter, how can you possibly have energy for a suggested activity? All right, if you insist, I suggest the activity of sitting quietly with a Buzzati cocktail and allowing no one to interrupt you until you say so.

SECTION NINE

Chapter **6**

Page 71

A brief summary of events: Victorious at last, King Leander and the bears burst into the Grand Theatre Excelsior to arrest the Grand Duke. Miraculously, Leander at last finds Tony, who has been forced to perform under an absurd name, but the Grand Duke cruelly cuts short the reunion by shooting Tony with an overdecorated weapon.

The lesson of this chapter is clear: There are few things more painful than a bad evening at the theater.

QUESTIONS YOU MAY FIND INTERESTING:

- As I'm sure you know, a landgraf is a German count who oversees small regions of land, usually farms. Yet Mr. Buzzati says he is "not quite sure what this is." Is he lying?
- Why would an Italian author lie about a German count who oversees small regions of land, usually farms? Doesn't that seem suspicious to you?
- Poor Tony must perform under the name

169

Bobadil. When you are kidnapped and forced into a theatrical life, what would be your least favorite stage name?

SUGGESTED ACTIVITY:

Recently I heard a rumor that the famous ballerinas of the Grand Theatre Excelsior, who turned to stone at the sight of the bears, will be taken down from the facade of the theater and will tour the world as part of a traveling display of interesting moments in history. Write down things you might like to see in such a display. I've taken the liberty of starting your list for you.

- The shoes that astronaut Neil Armstrong was wearing when he first stepped on the moon.
- A portrait of Violet Baudelaire, posing with many of her most famous inventions, painted by a former associate of mine.
- Several Egyptian mummies.
- An unusually large paper clip.
  Etcetera.

SECTION TEN

Chapter 7
Page 81

A brief summary of events: While everyone in the theater holds his or her breath, Professor Ambrose, inspired by the arrival of the dove of peace and goodwill, casts his last spell and rescues Tony from certain death. In celebration of this marvelous event—and of their victory in invading Sicily— the bears stage an enormous parade followed by an evening celebration.

The lesson of this chapter is clear: It is rare to see a truly unselfish act, but when you do, you ought to celebrate, making sure there are enough refreshments to go around.

QUESTIONS YOU MAY FIND INTERESTING:

- Do you think that Professor Ambrose actually used a magic wand to raise Tony from the dead, or is there another explanation?
- Do you think any details of this story have been changed, to make the book more interesting?
- If you look carefully at the illustration of the

171

dance in the park, you can see that the bears in the orchestra are sitting in the trees. Do you think it is safe for bears to perch in trees clutching heavy musical instruments? If not, how can we help them?

SUGGESTED ACTIVITY:

Observe your surroundings and watch carefully for an unselfish act. When this occurs, have an enormous party that lasts well into the evening. Of course, it would be very kind of you to extend an invitation to an author who is staying up well into the evening writing a reader's guide to be placed at the end of his favorite book.

SECTION ELEVEN

Chapter 8

Page 93

It is thirteen years later, although readers of this book do not have to wait thirteen years before beginning chapter eight. People and bears are living in peace, with Leander as their king, until a scandal erupts: Someone has stolen Professor Ambrose's new magic wand. Leander expresses his outrage to the men and women of his kingdom, but Ambrose suggests that the thief may not be a person at all.

The lesson of this chapter is clear: It is impolite to assume that one type of creature is more likely to be a criminal than another.

QUESTIONS YOU MAY FIND INTERESTING:

- The crowd is so alarmed by Leander's speech that one person throws a stone. At whom would you like to throw a stone?
- Mr. Buzzati makes a point of saying that Professor Ambrose is sneering, a word which here means "smiling or speaking in a way that

173

suggests you are not impressed with the person you're talking to." At whom would you like to sneer?

- Which do you think is worse to do, sneer or throw a stone? Which do you think is more satisfying?

SUGGESTED ACTIVITY:

In this chapter, King Leander stands on a balcony and makes a fierce speech in front of a captive audience, a phrase which here means "many people, all of whom are forced to listen to him." As the crowd's reaction shows us, it is best in these circumstances to carefully prepare what you are going to say. Write a fierce speech of your own, on any topic you find interesting, so that when you finally have your opportunity to talk to a captive audience you will avoid an angry riot.

174

SECTION TWELVE

Chapter *9*
Page 103

A brief summary of events: Professor Ambrose tells King Leander about a house of ill repute, a phrase which here means "enormous palace in which bears are drinking far too much wine," but when the King goes to investigate, he finds only Saltpetre living in a modest house. Before this mystery can be unraveled, however, it is discovered that the Universal Bank has been robbed. Ambrose is arrested, but a sharp-eyed bear named Dandelion suspects that the actual criminal has gone free.

The lesson of this chapter is clear: Things are seldom what they seem to be, including the lesson "things are seldom what they seem to be."

QUESTIONS YOU MAY FIND INTERESTING:

- The careful reader may suspect that there is more to Saltpetre's home than meets the eye. Is there more to your home than meets the eye?
- What would be the easiest way to find out if there were something suspicious going on in your own

175

home? (Hint: It involves staying up very late at night.)

• In the illustration of the Universal Bank, what is that large, round head in the sky? It certainly has a disturbing expression.

SUGGESTED ACTIVITY:

Most people think that alcoholic beverages, such as those served in Artichoke Park, ought to be enjoyed in moderation, a phrase which here means "by adults, as long as they do not drink too much and behave foolishly." You may prefer to drink nonalcoholic cocktails instead, particularly when dangerous things are happening around you and you need to be alert. Below is the recipe for the Buzzati Cocktail, a refreshing nonalcoholic beverage named in honor of the author of *The Bears' Famous Invasion of Sicily*:

The Buzzati Cocktail
1 sugar cube
$^1/_2$ lemon
$^1/_2$ teaspoon powdered ginger
tonic water
ice

176

Put the sugar cube in the bottom of a small glass. Chop the $1/2$ lemon into several slices, squeeze the juice into the glass, and drop the slices of lemon in. Add the ginger, and lightly mash all the ingredients together with a spoon until you have a mushy mixture in the bottom of the glass. (This is called a muddle, a word which also refers to individuals who are having trouble making decisions, like King Leander.) Add two or three ice cubes, and fill the glass with tonic water. Continue stirring your cocktail until it makes a very pleasing foam on top, and serve.

If you wish, you may alter the recipe to honor your favorite character in Buzzati's book. You may wish to consult the character list once more.

 If your favorite character is Leander, add $1/4$ teaspoon of honey, which the King always enjoys.

 If your favorite character is Professor Ambrose, add a few dashes of Angostura bitters, a liquid that is difficult to figure out, like the wizard himself.

 If your favorite character is the bear Titan, add a few extra ice cubes in honor of his giant snowballs.

 If your favorite character is the bear Merlin, add a maraschino cherry, which looks somewhat like the grenade he used to kill Marmoset the Cat.

 If your favorite character is the bear Marzipan, add a teaspoon of sliced, toasted almonds. Almonds are the principal ingredient in a sweet paste, also called Marzipan, which is almost as forgotten as the bears' history.

177

If your favorite character is the bear Theophilus (or any of the other apparitions), place the cocktail glass in the freezer for 1 minute or so before beginning the recipe. This will cause the glass to frost over, creating a ghostly setting for your beverage.

If your favorite character is the bear Dandelion, add a secret ingredient and make your guests discover what it is, in honor of Dandelion's detective skills.

If your favorite character is Tony, kidnap the lemon slices before serving, and hide them in a theater.

If your favorite character is the Screech-Owl, drink the cocktail in the middle of the night.

If your favorite character is the Old Man of the Mountains, drink the cocktail all by yourself.

If your favorite character is the bear Saltpetre, add $1/2$ cup of salt in honor of his salty name.*

If your favorite character is the Grand Duke, add 5 dashes of strong cologne in honor of his personal grooming habits.*

If your favorite character is Count Molfetta, add a slice of bacon in honor of his boars.*

If your favorite character is the Troll, add a small child to the cocktail, in honor of the Troll's favorite meal. You will probably need a larger glass.*

If your favorite character is Marmoset the Cat, the Sea Serpent, or the Werewolf, add a monstrous amount of black pepper.*

*These changes to the recipe will make the cocktail taste terrible,
but those who prefer such dreadful characters
will probably enjoy a dreadful beverage as well.*

178

SECTION THIRTEEN

Chapter *10*
Page 115

A brief summary of events: Alerted by a letter from Dandelion, King Leander bursts in on a gambling house, where to his horror he finds Tony. Enraged by the corruption in his kingdom, Leander confronts the citizens of Sicily, but Saltpetre manages to calm him down by proposing that a large statue of Leander be erected on top of a hill overlooking the city. But before the statue is finished, fishermen report that a monster has appeared.

The lesson of this chapter is clear: All of the joys and sorrows in the world can be forgotten in a moment if a sea serpent attacks.

QUESTIONS YOU MAY FIND INTERESTING:

- Dandelion's letter contains several major grammatical and spelling mistakes, and yet it finally convinces Leander of the serious problems in his kingdom. Does it matter if an important message contains these kind of errors?

179

- Do people ever point out minor errors in your own written work? What is to be done with such people?

SUGGESTED ACTIVITY:

Saltpetre distracts King Leander through flattery, a word which here means "excessively complimenting someone, even to the point of building a statue in his or her honor." Flattery is one of the most powerful forces in nature, and everyone would be wise to use it. Practice the art of flattery by trying the following exercises:

- Interrupt a relative who is yelling at you by complimenting their clothing or hair.
- When a teacher says something ridiculous to you, reply, "You are absolutely right. You are an absolutely brilliant person," and try to keep a straight face.
- When you break something that belongs to a friend, tell your friend that you were so distracted by his or her beauty, intelligence, and social charms that you lost your composure.

- Compose a long poem in honor of someone you scarcely know. Read the poem out loud in a dramatic voice. Then, ask that person for an enormous favor and see what happens.
- When someone you don't like enters the room, bow.
- When someone is rude to you, burst into overdramatic tears and say, "Even one unkind word from someone as wonderful as you shatters my heart into a million pieces." Keep wailing until they apologize.

SECTION FOURTEEN

Chapter 11

Page 127

A brief summary of events: Reading this chapter will likely make you gasp in pain several times in a row, as if you are falling down a short but sharp-edged flight of stairs. First, King Leander bravely faces the sea serpent and manages to destroy the creature with a harpoon . . . just as the treacherous Saltpetre shoots the King, hoping the crime will look like an accident in the confusion. But Dandelion, who always suspected Saltpetre of terrible things, realizes at once what has happened, and executes the criminal on the spot. All in all it is a terrible afternoon.

The lesson of this chapter is clear: When you are facing a monster, it is impossible to watch your back.

QUESTIONS YOU MAY FIND INTERESTING:

- Traditionally, criminals are arrested and go through a judicial process. Instead, Dandelion immediately cuts off Saltpetre's head. Which method of justice do you prefer?

182

- Traditionally, wild beasts are captured and taken to remote locations. Instead, Leander kills the serpent with a harpoon. Which method of justice do you prefer?
- Examine the illustration. You will notice that the men and women seem to be on one side of town, and the bears on the other. Why do you think this is?

SUGGESTED ACTIVITY:

Many events in this story can be linked together to make a sort of chain. For instance, if Tony had not been kidnapped, the bears might not have invaded Sicily. If the bears had not invaded Sicily, Saltpetre might not have wanted to be king himself. If Saltpetre had not wanted to be king himself, Leander might not have been murdered. If Leander had not been murdered, Saltpetre would not have been executed. Write down a chain of events in your own life, and try to imagine what would happen if you changed one link in the chain.

SECTION FIFTEEN

Chapter 12
Page 135

A brief summary of events: On his deathbed, King Leander asks the bears to give up the ways of men, abandon the city, and return to the mountains. They obey, leaving behind everything. Only the unfinished statue survives, where it apparently survives to this day.

The lesson of this chapter is clear: The bears' famous invasion of Sicily, like so many things in life, turns out to be scarcely worthwhile, with much tragedy and treachery on the way, with many horrifying detours, and finally a melancholy ending, full of death and sadness, that fades over years and years and leaves scarcely anything for people to remember. It must be said, however, that starving to death in the mountains wouldn't have been fun either.

QUESTIONS YOU MAY FIND INTERESTING:

- Traditionally, whatever is said on one's deathbed must be obeyed. What are you planning to say on your deathbed?
- "No one is indispensable in this world," Leander says, using a word which here means "absolutely

184

necessary" or "impossible to replace." Do you agree with him? Are you indispensable? What about me? Am I indispensable? (Remember the previous activity regarding flattery.)

SUGGESTED ACTIVITY:

Gather your friends and comrades,
And meet them someplace dark,
Like an abandoned notebook factory,
Or a lonely, shady park.

Hatch a plan to conquer
A land you do not like.
Gather food and weapons,
And set off on your hike.

Battle all the monsters,
Bury several friends.
Comfort those who say to you,
"The anguish never ends!"

Yes, you'll win the conflict,
And rule for many years,
But your kingdom will be covered
In trouble and in tears.

More monsters will attack you,
And not just from outside,
In the hearts of certain friends
Much treachery will hide.

What terrible confusion
Has your invasion brought?
Has some moral come to light,
A lesson to be taught?

But now your life is over.
You have only one last breath.
You tell your friends to go back home
As you await your death.

So much pain has come your way,
So much bloodshed, so much crime.
But still when all is said and done:
It was an interesting time.